The thief studied Slocum's face for a full minute, then said slowly, "Damned if I don't believe you. But you got to know the risk I'm takin'."

"I'll do as I promised."

"Ain't no love 'tween Innick and the marshal, that's for sure. And you and the marshal don't get on too good either."

"I couldn't care less about the marshal or Innick. I'm being paid to do a job—breaking you out is part of it."

"There was this fellow. He was the one who put me up to the robbery in the first place. He was dressed like he was from a circus."

Slocum remembered the storekeeper's description. Purple velvet coat, brocade vest, silk pants. "Only he wasn't from a circus," Slocum said. "You said he told you about the jewelry?"

"He had it all planned out. A real thinker, he was. I did like he told me, and I waltzed away with everything. And that was the strange part. He only wanted that ruby. The rest he let me keep. He ran his finger over that ruby like he was fondlin' a whore's tit."

The jailhouse's outer door creaked open. Slocum caught a glimpse of the marshal and dropped out of sight.

"You promised!" the thief called.

And Slocum had. First he wanted to be sure about this peacock of a criminal mastermind.

JAKE LOGAN

SLOCUM AND THE YELLOWSTONE SCOUNDREL

JOVE BOOKS, NEW YORK

THE BERKLEY PUBLISHING GROUP
Published by the Penguin Group
Penguin Group (USA) Inc.
375 Hudson Street, New York, New York 10014, USA

USA | Canada | UK | Ireland | Australia | New Zealand | India | South Africa | China

Penguin Books Ltd., Registered Offices: 80 Strand, London WC2R 0RL, England
For more information about the Penguin Group, visit penguin.com.

SLOCUM AND THE YELLOWSTONE SCOUNDREL

A Jove Book / published by arrangement with the author

Jove Books are published by The Berkley Publishing Group.
JOVE® is a registered trademark of Penguin Group (USA) Inc.
The "J" design is a trademark of Penguin Group (USA) Inc.

For information, address: The Berkley Publishing Group,
a division of Penguin Group (USA) Inc.,
375 Hudson Street, New York, New York 10014.

ISBN: 978-0-515-15313-2

PUBLISHING HISTORY
Jove mass-market edition / May 2013

PRINTED IN THE UNITED STATES OF AMERICA

10 9 8 7 6 5 4 3 2 1

Cover illustration by Sergio Giovine.

1

"Get back!"

John Slocum's warning came an instant too late. Blood sprayed upward and over him. He recoiled, threw up his bare arm, and tried to keep the blood from his eyes. He failed. The world went black around him as Joe Reese's blood blinded him. Rubbing furiously, he made his eyes water. Cries of utter anguish made it even more important for him to see clearly.

Reese's moans lost their shrill, frightened sound and turned to whimpers.

"Get some help over here!" Slocum shouted. His words were snuffed out by the whine of the sawmill blades chewing through shaved tree trunks to turn out ten-foot-long planks of rough-cut wood.

"Slocum, help me! Gettin' so cold," Reese sobbed out. "Can't hardly feel nuthin'." The man moved, trying to reach out for aid. His arm had been severed just above the elbow so all he did was point his stump in Slocum's direction.

Slocum fumbled around and found where he had cast off his flannel shirt in the heat of the sawmill and used the sleeve to wipe the other man's blood from his face. Blurred images came, and then he saw where Reese lay at the foot of the still spinning silver blade.

How it had happened didn't matter because nothing now would change the fact that Reese had lost most of his right arm to the huge, spinning saw blade. The spurts of blood from the stump just below the shoulder were diminishing. Slocum knew what that meant. Joe Reese wasn't long for this world.

He dropped to his knees beside the man. He pushed him back flat onto the sawdust-covered floor.

"Lay still," Slocum snapped. He whipped the sleeve of his shirt around the bloody stump, tied it tight, then found a small branch on the floor. He shoved it between shirt and flesh, then began turning. The tourniquet cut off the tiny blood flow and squeezed down on the stump, threatening to slide off as the skin compressed all the way down to bone.

Slocum had to readjust it to keep the pressure on. Reese's blood still oozed out in a gory mix of flesh, dirt, and wood chips. As long as he bled, he lived.

"What are you two goldbricks doing? Get your asses back to work!"

Slocum ignored the foreman, Hank Tomasson. He leaned forward and gave the tourniquet another twist. Reese had gone pale, and his lips were turning fat and blue. A minute earlier his face had turned a deathly gray.

"What the hell happened?"

"Get him some help," Slocum said. "This isn't working. He's lost too much blood to—"

He rocked back on his heels and released the tourniquet. Blood dripped from the stump. If Reese was still alive, even with a feebly beating heart, there would have been a renewed spurt.

"He's lost it all," the foreman said. "Ain't no more to leak out. Damnation. What am I gonna tell the boss? That we're a hand shy?"

Slocum looked up, his vision still fuzzed. Tomasson held the severed arm aloft as if it might bite him.

"You don't go nowhere, Slocum," the foreman said. Bellowing to be heard above the din, Tomasson brought half a dozen other men running.

Slocum sat cross-legged in the sawdust, staring at Tomasson and the arm in the man's hand. As the foreman finally realized he still held it, he threw the appendage away onto a heap of wood scrap.

"I tole that stupid son of a bitch to keep his arms free of the blade. That wheel's a man killer, for certain sure."

"Looks like his sleeve got caught on a blade tooth and that pulled him in," Slocum said.

"Wasn't hot enough for him to take off his shirt, I reckon. He shoulda worked hard enough to break a sweat. His loss," Tomasson said.

Slocum picked up his shirt and tried to worry out the knot he had tied in the sleeve. The drying blood made that hard. He turned from the body and started out of the sawmill.

"Where you goin', Slocum? You get on back here now, you hear? There's still work to be done!"

Slocum heard. He didn't care. He had labored at the sawmill on Otter Creek for the better part of a month after drifting north from Salt Lake City. The Wasatch Mountains in spring didn't hold much in the way of employment, but he had been lucky to get the job here. Samuel Innick had bought the land and equipment and needed an entire crew when the old one quit as a man, refusing to work for him. Slocum had worked as a lumberjack in the Pacific Northwest a few years earlier, but his experience around the immense blades had gotten him a plum job making twice what a man with an ax could out in the woods.

He went to the creek and flopped forward, thrust his head under the rapidly flowing cold, crystal water, then sputtered when he couldn't hold his breath any longer. Dipping his shirt in the frigid river was more likely to set the stains than clean them, but he was past caring. He heard the commotion up in the mill, even over the whup-whup of the turning waterwheel powering the saw blades.

He scraped at the clotted blood and beat his shirt on the rocks. The blood hadn't set, not entirely, and he got most of it out. After wringing it as dry as he could, he put it on. The day was warm, but the clammy flannel next to his skin made him shiver.

"Slocum, the boss wants to see you." Tomasson wasn't a man to mince words. For that, Slocum was glad. Pussyfooting around what was likely to come didn't suit him one little bit. They wanted someone to blame for Reese's death, and he had been there.

Case closed.

He got to his feet and took a deep breath. It did nothing to calm him. He had seen men wounded worse during the war, but so much blood and death weren't a part of his everyday life now. Not for a spell.

Plodding back up the steep slope, he started for the mill but Tomasson pointed in the opposite direction.

"Mr. Innick's office. He sounded real upset."

"Do tell," Slocum said. From back at the mill came the sounds of men laughing and joking about how dumb Joe Reese had been.

Their humor disgusted him. Reese had been careless, and it had cost him his life. There wasn't any call for them to rag on him now. Slocum went to the small cabin where the mill owner kept the books, hired and fired, and passed out the pay every two weeks.

Slocum was a week from getting more money. He wasn't sure he could afford to lose that much pay, but the only reason Innick would have to see him was to fire him. Blame him for Reese's death, chew him out for not instructing the man better, simply vent his own frustration at losing an employee. Slocum didn't know. What he did know was that the shock was wearing off and a cold fury was building. His hand touched his left hip. He didn't bother wearing his Colt Navy slung in its cross-draw holster while working. It would only get in his way.

He had to retrieve it from the bunkhouse before riding on. Going southwest toward Salt Lake City didn't appeal much to him. The Mormons weren't inclined to let a man kill the aches and pains of being in the saddle too long with a shot of whiskey. They certainly didn't cotton to the notion of a man needing the comfort that only a woman could offer unless there was marriage involved. Better that he ride north a ways to Sage Creek Junction, get what supplies he could, and press on into Wyoming or north even farther to Montana. There had to be a horse rancher in need of a wrangler.

About all the money he had in his jeans was left from the last pay he'd received. Slocum doubted it amounted to more than four dollars, and most of that in greenbacks issued on a local bank. Leave the area and nobody else would touch that paper money.

The cabin door stood ajar. Slocum pushed it open all the way and waited until Innick noticed him. The mill owner impatiently motioned him inside.

"Close the door, Slocum." Innick frowned. "You fall into the millrace or something?"

Slocum said nothing. This wasn't going the way he had anticipated.

"Set yourself down." Innick scowled as Slocum sank into a chair, then said, "You got the look of a man who can use a six-shooter."

"I can."

"Thought so from the condition of your iron. Looked worn, used but cared for."

"I didn't shoot Reese," he said.

Innick's eyebrows shot up in surprise. He started to say something, then sagged a little.

"Damned mill. Everything falls on my shoulders at the same time. Tomasson let me know about the accident. A shame, a damned shame. Now, you willing to earn a reward?"

"You pay for Reese's burial?"

"I don't—is that part of your price?"

"What do you want from me?" Slocum knew they could dance around whatever was eating at Innick, and he was in no mood for that.

"I've been robbed. My wife's jewelry was stolen, and I want you to track down the man who took it."

"I'm not a lawman," Slocum said. The notion of wearing a badge turned him cold.

More than once he had crossed the line of legality and taken part in bank and stage robberies. It had been a year and longer since that had been the only way to earn money, but if Innick hadn't given him the sawmill job, he would have been interested in snatching his wife's jewelry for the paltry few dollars it would get him.

"Don't want a lawman, want a bounty hunter."

"I'm not a bounty hunter either." Slocum had been pursued by those relentless men more than once, coming after him for a dispute over land back in Georgia.

He had been gut shot and left for dead toward the end of the war. Recuperating on the family farm in Calhoun, Georgia, had taken long, lonely months since his parents were dead and his brother had died during Pickett's Charge. A carpetbagger judge had decided to steal the farm using forged documents. Slocum hadn't been agreeable. He'd buried the judge and his hired gunman by the springhouse, then rode on.

He hated bounty hunters more than he did lawmen. They usually held on to an old wanted poster with his likeness on it on the off chance their wanderings might bring him into their gun sights. Killing a federal judge, even a thieving carpetbagger judge, had dogged his heels ever since.

"Look, Slocum, I'm offering you five hundred dollars to get back my wife's jewelry. She got most of it from her ma and grandma. It's worth a tidy sum, but her family history's worth far more."

Slocum simply stared. Five hundred dollars was more than he had seen in the entire past year. Innick mistook his look.

"Five hundred and seeing your partner isn't buried in the potter's field."

"Reese? Yeah, good." Slocum's mind raced. "Why not let the marshal look into this? You suspect him of being the crook?"

"I knew I'd picked the right man," Innick said. "Me and Marshal Smith don't get on very well. His people come from Scotland, mine from Ireland. Bad blood stretches back all the way to the Emerald Isle."

"When was the theft?"

"Last night, best we can tell. The missus went to put on a cameo broach and the entire box was empty. Gold chains, precious stones set in rings and bracelets, heirlooms."

"How much would all this weigh? Could the crook have stuffed it into a coat pocket without being noticed?"

"I see how you're thinking, Slocum. He could. A large pocket would hold it all. Or saddlebags. Who'd notice a man walking around here with saddlebags slung over his shoulder?"

"Anyone missing?"

Innick turned to stone.

"I searched everyone's belongings. Nothing was stashed in the bunkhouse."

"That how you came around to the idea I knew how to use my Colt?" Slocum read the answer on the man's face. This was exactly what had happened. While he sifted through everyone's belongings looking for the stolen loot, he had found Slocum's ebony-handled Colt Navy, a six-gun that wouldn't be out of place in the grip of a gunslinger.

"I'm offering a lot of money."

"How do you know you can trust me?"

"The jewelry's not worth five hundred dollars, that's how. You stand to make a hell of a lot more by being honest." Innick paused, then said, looking Slocum squarely in the eye, "I can read men pretty good. You might cut corners, but you keep your word. If you promised to do the job, you'd do it honestly."

"I need to look around the place where the jewelry was kept. There might be a chance I can track whoever stole it."

"A good idea. That never occurred to me. Come along."

Innick shot from his chair and almost bowled Slocum over as he hurried from the cabin and started climbing the steps cut into the side of the hill leading to the house perched on top. Slocum shivered as he followed. The drying flannel shirt reminded him of how quickly Joe Reese had died. At least Innick would see to the man's funeral.

"You need to see inside the house?"

Slocum heard the warning in the man's voice. Poking about inside would upset his wife even more by reminding her of the theft, and that was the last thing in the world he wanted.

"Show me the window of the room. Bedroom?"

Innick nodded and started around the house. The soft earth compressed with every footstep Slocum took. He was glad there hadn't been any rain for a couple days. There might be a chance he could find a decent boot imprint. He reached out and grabbed Innick's arm, stopping him before the man could stand directly under the window. The mill owner bristled, then realized why Slocum had touched him.

"You don't need me pawing around on the ground, ruining the tracks. Sorry."

The apology surprised Slocum. He realized then how serious the matter was to Innick—or more likely, his wife. Approaching the area directly under the window with the utmost caution, Slocum saw how the grass had been crushed and broken. Deep indentations showed that someone had jumped from the window ledge and had landed hard. He ran his forefinger around the print.

"What can you tell from doing that?"

"The gent wasn't wearing spurs but had boots. And there's a large notch in the right heel. He might have stomped down on something sharp and cut it out or the boot might be so old the sole is starting to fall off."

"Why can't you tell?"

Slocum looked up and tried to keep the contempt from his voice. This man had offered him five hundred dollars. And a funeral.

"The dirt shows the cut, not the age of the boots." He pushed back some of the bent grass and showed Innick what he had found.

"Find a man wearing a boot with a notch cut in the right heel and you got your man. Very good, Slocum. You're a hell of a tracker."

Slocum already paced alongside the tracks. A blind man could have followed them to where a horse had been tethered. From here it was an easy ride to the road leading to town. While the thief might have hightailed it, Slocum doubted that had happened. Gold jewelry wasn't worth much unless it could be sold or melted down. Either of those might be available in town but not on the trail. If he had stolen the jewelry, he would have wanted to get rid of it as fast as he could.

"I'll have Tomasson saddle your horse and bring it around. You think you can fetch it back? The jewelry?"

Slocum nodded.

"Good. I'll have your money waiting for you."

"I'll want a decent tombstone on the grave," Slocum said.

"This dead fellow, Reese. He was your partner?"

"No," Slocum said, then turned away. He didn't want to explain that doing the right thing ought to be second nature. For him it was. For Innick, not so much.

2

Slocum rode slowly into the town of Otter Creek. The first time he had gone down the main street, he felt as if everyone eyed him, knowing he didn't have two nickels to rub together. Now he was sure rifles were trained on him, the thief ready to kill him from ambush. He tried to shake off the paranoia as an aftereffect of seeing Joe Reese die so suddenly and spectacularly.

He wasn't sure that was all. Being a bounty hunter didn't set well with him, but the lure of enough money to ride on and leave behind the sawmill and the petty tyrants like Tomasson appealed to him.

Drawing rein in front of the saloon, he looked inside to see a half-dozen men bellied up to the bar. They paid him no attention. A slow look around the street showed nobody paid him any heed. He stepped down, wrapped the reins around an iron ring mounted on a post, and went into the saloon. Finding out who the likely thief was required him to gather information. Men drinking heavily provided the easiest way of doing it—and didn't require him to skin his knuckles beating the information out of anyone.

"Beer," he said.

"You're off work early," the bartender said. She was a short, stout woman of indeterminate age with graying hair pulled back in an unattractive bun that bristled with a comb and silver spines, making her look like a human cactus. Slocum figured she didn't want to be too appealing to her customers since she wasn't a bad-looking woman.

"Need to find a varmint who was working out at the mill," he said slowly.

The barkeep's dark eyes hardened.

"Do tell." She drew the beer and slid it in front of him.

"He stole damned near ten dollars from my saddlebags. Took a photograph, too. Meant the world to me." Slocum lied easily, staring into the thin ring of white foam on the amber beer. He saw that a claim of stealing money meant nothing to the woman, but the photograph struck a chord.

"Family?"

Slocum nodded.

"Some folks'll steal anything that's not nailed down, and if it is, they'll steal the nails, too. What's the thief look like?"

"Somebody just passing through town, I reckon. Not even worth telling the marshal."

"Wouldn't do much good to bother Marshal Smith anyway. Son of a buck's never sober." The way she said that caused Slocum to perk up.

"Sober enough to ride?"

The woman laughed ruefully and shook her head.

"Falls out of the saddle. Haven't seen him astride a horse in months. Hemorrhoids, he says. I don't think there's a horse in all of Utah that'd let him set across its back and not protest the weight."

She let out a tiny snort and called, "Your ears burnin', Marshal? I was just tellin' this fellow how good a lawman you are."

Slocum looked up behind the bar into the mirror. Reflected was about the fattest man he had ever laid eyes on. From the scene of the robbery and how the thief had gone through a window, agilely jumping down and then briskly walking away, this wasn't his man. Slocum had tried to guess the thief's weight by the depth of the boot impression and couldn't. If this man had dropped from the window ledge, the imprint would have gone halfway to the center of the earth. Marshal Smith waddled to a table and dropped into a chair, puffing from the exertion.

"Shut up, Maggie, and fetch me a beer. My feet are burning and my throat's all parched."

"I'll take it to him," Slocum said, intercepting the beer mug. "Got to talk to him anyway." Slocum and the barkeep's eyes met. She relented. It was obvious Maggie didn't care one whit for the marshal.

Slocum set the mug down on the table and saw how the marshal had hiked his feet onto a chair. He cast a quick look at the heels. They were worn but otherwise intact. He doubted Smith had a second pair with a notch cut out of one heel he used only for thieving purposes. From the look of his clothing, the marshal wore all he owned, probably not even having Sunday-go-to-meeting clothes.

"You the new bouncer here?"

"Just passing through," Slocum said as he settled down into the chair opposite the lawman.

From behind the bar, Maggie called out, "He was robbed. Up at Innick's sawmill. Some son of a bitch stole a picture of his family."

Smith looked at him with bloodshot eyes. He obviously wanted to be somewhere else so he wouldn't have to listen to news of any crime, but the lure of the beer proved too great. He grunted as he bent forward and snared the mug. He lifted it to his lips and drained it in one noisy gulp, then clicked it back to the table. Beer foam turned his greasy brown mustache momentarily white. Then it soaked in to join the rest of everything the marshal had eaten and drunk that day—or maybe for the prior week.

"No value to a photograph," the marshal said. "You're outta luck."

"Some money was taken, too," Slocum said, "but the picture was special. You come across any sneak thieves the past day or two? Ones that might have hightailed it from town?"

"Well, now, let me ponder on that subject." Smith made a production out of licking his lips and wiping his mustache, looking from the mug to Slocum and back.

Slocum took the hint and bought the lawman another beer, then settled back down in the chair opposite. Smith knocked back the second beer as fast as he had the first. This time a loud belch accompanied the slurping.

"Now that you mention it, there was one gent acting real squirrelly. Came to town from the direction of that no-account Innick's mill."

Slocum got the message that the marshal and Innick weren't the best of friends, which verified the mill owner's story as to why he hadn't bothered notifying the marshal of the jewelry theft. Even a shot of whiskey in way of a bribe wouldn't budge his fat ass to investigate a crime at the mill.

"What'd he look like?"

"Didn't pay a whole lot of attention. Looked like a weasel. Eyes always darting around, like somebody was dogging his steps. Saw a gambler like that once. Somebody was after him. Shot him in the back."

"Which way did this weasel ride from town?"

"North, no west," he hastily corrected. "He went west. Thought that was strange since he cut across country and didn't look to be following the road that'd take him to Logan. You haven't missed him by more 'n an hour. Two. Hung around, like he was waitin' fer somethin'."

Slocum considered that the marshal might be sending him on a wild-goose chase, then asked, "Did he try to sell anything in town?"

"Why'd anybody want a damned picture? What was it?

One of them blue photographs of a dancing girl? All nekkid or maybe not wearing too much? I can see why you'd want to steal a picture like that. I can understand why Innick would have one. You ever see that harridan of a wife he married? Ugly as sin."

"Thanks, Marshal," Slocum said, getting to his feet.

"You get that there picture back, you let me look at it, won't you?"

Slocum left without so much as a backward glance. He went into the street and slowly studied the stores, then set out for the general store. The wizened man in an apron behind the counter looked up.

"Afternoon, son. What can I get for you?"

"You sell jewelry? Real special gold jewelry?"

"Well, now, can't say that I do," the man said, scowling. "Funny you should ask. Not an hour back a man came in trying to sell me some necklaces and bracelets and the like. No market for that. I suggested he try selling them in Salt Lake City. More women folk likely to appreciate such baubles."

"He didn't say anything about wanting to melt them down?"

"He didn't. Nobody in town could do work like that. Maybe the blacksmith but he's out east of town. His wife's ma was serious sick, so he drove the missus over in the buggy a couple days back."

"Thanks," Slocum said.

"Don't know what his partner thought."

"His partner?" Slocum looked harder at the storekeeper.

"Gaudiest peacock of a man I ever did see. Brocade vest, all gold and green. His coat looked to be velvet. Purple, it was. Couldn't see his trousers too good, but they had a silky look to 'em. He didn't come into the store with the fellow peddling the jewelry, but I knowed they was together. They talked for a few minutes after I turned him down."

"He didn't come in with the one who looked like a weasel?"

"You know him, then. That's perzactly the way he looked. Like a weasel. Not even a decent marmot or other rodent. A weasel."

"Rode west when he left? Both of them?"

"Can't say about the clotheshorse. The man with the jewelry went west, as you said." The storekeeper cocked his head to one side, closed an eye to better focus on Slocum, then asked, "You a lawman? That varmint—the weasel—had the look of a sneak thief. Who'd he steal the gold from?"

When Slocum didn't answer, the shopkeeper went on. He sniffed once, then nodded, as if everything was explained.

"I do think he stole the jewelry from Sean Innick's wife. The man who owns the sawmill. I smell fresh-cut wood on your clothes, so you're likely one of Innick's boys. Mrs. Innick always goes on about how much her jewelry cost. She must have saved it for special occasions and nobody in town's never gonna be special enough to see it."

"Did his partner ride with him, you think?"

"As I said, don't know that. The peacock didn't look like he was a horse-riding man, not in them fancy britches."

Slocum left, wondering what he ought to do. A second man so opulently dressed would be easier to find, but he had never been seen with the weasel, who had tried to sell the stolen jewelry. For all the clerk knew, the dandy had been asked for directions and had no other connection. But Slocum didn't believe that. He couldn't.

He swung into the saddle and rode straight from town, going west. At first he thought his hunt would be futile, then he saw how the sloping land funneled down to a large ravine. Anyone leaving town likely came this way rather than fighting to ride along either rocky bank.

After less than an hour of riding, Slocum spotted fresh horse dung. Luck stayed with him as found tracks in the ravine bottom that couldn't have been more than an hour old from the sharp impressions around the horseshoe print.

Wind and sun would have baked them until they began to crumble within a few hours.

When the rider he pursued left the ravine, heading southward, Slocum had a trail so obvious that a blind man could follow it. As he trotted along, he drew his Colt Navy and made sure it was loaded. Then he pulled an old Henry rifle from the saddle sheath and checked the magazine. The tubular magazine was filled with sixteen rounds of the .44-caliber rimfire ammo. Slocum was ready to take on an army.

From the description of the man he pursued, he doubted anything more than the threat of being shot would be necessary to learn what he wanted and maybe even get back the stolen jewelry.

As dusk settled like a cool blanket, Slocum slowed, then dismounted to keep the tracks in view. A rocky patch forced him to use a bit more of his skill, but not too much. Bright scratch marks here and there on the rock left by the steel horseshoes proved more than enough to keep him moving.

By the time he sniffed the air and caught the pinewood smoke and a hint of coffee brewing, he knew he had found his quarry.

The dancing flames showed through a screen of underbrush ahead. Slocum considered how best to approach the man. He didn't know for certain if he had the right trail, but he thought he did. Riding in, gun drawn, might be advisable, but he didn't want to spook the man into fighting.

Slocum found a game trail and walked forward slowly, stopping at the edge of the clearing where the man had made his camp.

Slocum called out, "Howdy! I'm traveling through and don't mean you any harm."

The man jerked up, his hand reaching for something shoved into his belt. Slocum made a mental note of that. No holster, but the man was armed. Probably his weapon was a smaller caliber than a .44 to rest easy in the waistband of his pants.

"Mind if I share some of my grub with you? I can swap some fresh beef for that coffee. That smells mighty fine, by the way."

"Come on over," the man said, shifting so his hand was hidden under his coat. Slocum had no doubt the man gripped the handle of his pistol so tight his hand might be shaking soon enough.

"Been on the trail since before sunup," Slocum said. "You see the Indians?"

"Injuns? What Injuns?" The man turned and faced Slocum. Even if Marshal Smith and the shop owner hadn't branded the man as a weasel, the thought would have taken immediate form and been foremost out of Slocum's lips.

His face was narrow, eyes deep-set and dark. Huge bushy eyebrows and greasy strands of hair almost hid his forehead. His angular face turned into a snout as the campfire light flickered.

"Here you go," Slocum said, tossing over his saddlebags.

The man grabbed with both hands. Slocum stepped over and snared the pistol thrust into the man's waistband. As he had guessed, it was a small pistol, hardly worth the name. At close range it was more likely to set a man's shirt on fire than to kill him, but it was the sort of pistol Slocum expected from such a man.

"You cain't rob me!" the thief whined. That grated on Slocum's nerves enough to make him consider shooting the man with his own gun. Instead, he merely cocked and pointed it between the man's eyes.

"Where's the jewelry you stole?"

"H-How'd you know?"

"The man you stole from is powerful pissed off. You're lucky I found you and not one of the others."

"The others?" The man's eyes went wide. "What others is that?"

"Why, Innick's got a dozen men hunting for you. All of 'em work at his sawmill and promised Innick they'd run you through the blades, one piece at a time, unless you returned his wife's jewelry." Slocum wanted to scare the thief enough to get what he wanted without having to resort to more drastic measures.

"You ain't one of them lumberjacks?"

"I prefer other work."

"Me and you, we can split the—" The man blanched when he saw Slocum's expression as he tried to dicker. Up until now Slocum had been inclined to let the man go if he just forked over the stolen goods. Seeing he was as crooked as a dog's hind leg, Slocum knew the man deserved to be in jail.

"Where is it? In your saddlebags?"

Slocum didn't look at the worn leather bags but kept his eyes on the man. The small twist to his body, the quick dart of the eyes, and then a return as if he realized how he betrayed himself, told the story.

"You bury the goods?"

"Just for the night. Don't want no sneak thief robbin' me whilst I slept."

Slocum said, "You can't cheat an honest man."

This brought forth a loud snort.

"Hell, them's the ones with the most money. Till I get done with 'em."

"How'd you come to rob Innick?"

"His wife came into town for Sunday services flashin' her gold bracelets and fancy necklace. Caused a wave of gossip since she don't usually show off the glittery jewels that much, or so the old biddies in the church said. Something special comin' up. She even had pearls all wove up in her hair. How could any man resist stealin' a treasure trove like that?"

"Yeah, how could anybody?" Slocum glanced toward the spot where the thief had foolishly allowed his gaze to go and saw a pile of rocks that didn't look natural. He used the captured pistol to motion the thief to the pile. "You move a few of those rocks and show me what's under them."

"How'd you—" The man bit off the question. He began to understand how he had been outmaneuvered to this point.

The obvious shift in the weasel-faced man's demeanor put Slocum on guard. He kept back a few paces and was glad. The first rock the man pulled from the pile came sailing at him. Slocum easily dodged the missile.

"If you don't keep this pistol in good condition, let me assure you mine is in perfect condition." Slocum turned slightly to thrust his left hip forward to display his Colt. "The next thing I see coming my way had better be everything you stole."

Slocum saw the man's reaction and wondered. The thief tensed, as if he considered running. Something about the mention of what had been stolen made the thief especially edgy.

"It's here. All I got's here."

Slocum let the man paw through the rocks and pull out a leather pouch. When he held it up over his head, Slocum grabbed it away. By the light from the nearby campfire, he saw the glitter of gold inside.

He tugged on the leather cord and said, "Get your gear. We're going back to town."

"But you got the loot. Let me go!"

"I'll let the marshal decide what to do with you. Now break camp and let's ride."

They rode into town, exhausted, just after dawn. He turned over the thief to Marshal Smith and then headed back to the sawmill to collect what might have been the easiest five hundred he had ever earned.

3

Slocum stood in front of Innick's desk in the small cabin, balancing the leather pouch in his hand as the man scrabbled to find the reward money. Innick looked up, then returned to the hunt, muttering as he rooted about through drawers.

"Didn't expect you to get back so quick, Slocum," the sawmill owner said. "I would have had your money."

"The marshal said there wasn't a reward for bringing him in." Slocum had hoped the thief had a wanted poster out on him. Such a theft couldn't have been his first excursion into lawlessness. He had committed the robbery too skillfully for Slocum to believe that.

Slocum hadn't asked, but he knew that after the weasely thief had seen Mrs. Innick strutting about with her jewelry at church, he had shown a considerable amount of restraint not robbing her on her way home. He might have broken into the Innick bedroom more than once to be sure the jewelry was there. Slocum couldn't imagine luck had entered into the theft, all the precious metal and gemstones resting in the box at the same instant.

"Here," Innick said, finding a checkbook. He began to write.

"I want cash," Slocum said. "No check."

"You can cash it in town. I'm good for it. Hell, man, I *own* the town. Without the sawmill, there wouldn't be so much as a widening in the road at Otter Creek."

"Money, not a check," Slocum said, tossing the leather pouch from hand to hand. The threat was obvious, and Innick's normally florid face turned beet red.

"You cannot keep the jewelry! I paid to have you return it!"

Before Slocum could say a word, he felt a breeze at his back as the door opened.

"Oh, Sean, give him the money. Is that my jewelry?" A quick, stubby-fingered hand festooned with rings caught the leather bag with the speed of a striking snake.

Mrs. Innick pushed past Slocum and spread out the stolen merchandise on her husband's desk. She pawed through it.

"You've done well, sir," she said. "I appreciate your daring and bringing the crook to such swift justice."

Slocum looked from the matron to Innick. The man's face turned a shade redder, then he closed the checkbook and reached into an inner coat pocket to pull out a wallet thick with banknotes. He began counting them out. Slocum would have preferred gold or silver coins, but notes written on a Salt Lake City bank would do. He had seen merchants throughout the region accepting the paper.

"Thanks," Slocum said, rolling the bills into a wad that disappeared into his coat pocket. He had enough to move on. But there was one further matter to finish. "The funeral?"

"For Reese? He's buried up on the top of the hill, overlooking the sawmill."

Slocum waited for more.

"All right, he got a fancy pine box from wood sawed right here. Tomasson found one of the men was a preacher. He said words."

Slocum nodded, turned to go, and then froze when Mrs. Innick let out a screech that cut to his soul.

"It's not here! It's gone! My mama's precious ruby is missing! See!" She held up a pendant. The gold prongs had been pried away to leave a hollow center.

"Must be in the bag," Innick said uneasily. He started pawing through the jewelry spread on the desk, then patted the leather pouch and finally peered into it as if the mere act of inspection would cause the missing ruby to appear.

"You did not bring back the ruby!" Mrs. Innick looked accusingly at Slocum.

"That's all there was to bring back," Slocum said. "I didn't take anything."

"Not saying you did, Slocum, not at all," Innick said uneasily. "But this thief, the one in jail, he might have hid it or sold it. Hell, he might still have it."

Slocum doubted that. Marshal Smith would have searched his prisoner. If the ruby had been on the thief, the marshal had it now.

"Might be so," Slocum said carefully, "but when I turned him over to the law, the marshal proved reluctant to hold him."

"Because it was my property that had been stolen," Innick said.

"*My* property," Mrs. Innick said tartly. "Mr. Slocum seems an honorable man. He could have ridden away with all the jewelry if he had fancied himself a thief."

"That's so," Innick said, a dark cloud descending now on him. "Smith might have taken it off the thief, if the man had tucked it into a pocket. He hates me. He'd think this was only his due after that business with his house being foreclosed." Innick shoved to his feet. "I'll beard the old lion in his den and demand its return!"

"You'll do no such thing, Sean," Mrs. Innick said. "You would lose your temper, and my mama's ruby would be lost forever. You know I intended to gift it to Lauren on the date of her wedding."

"I can make the marshal—"

"You can't make him do a thing after you had him thrown out of his house. He sleeps in the jail now." She turned and looked up at Slocum. "Let this young man fetch the ruby. He has done well so far. Let him earn his money and get *all* my property back. And you must hurry. My daughter and her beau are getting married next month. I will not have their life together blighted by not presenting Lauren with the ruby." With that, Mrs. Innick held up the pendant that had once carried the ruby as its centerpiece, then flounced from the small office. She slammed the door behind her with a sound that might have been the peal of doom.

Slocum waited for Innick to demand back the reward money he had already paid. For a moment the men stared down each other. Innick blinked. Getting his money back from Slocum wasn't going to happen, not with the Colt Navy slung low on Slocum's left hip in its cross-draw holster. If the sawmill owner called for Tomasson and any of his crew, men would die.

And Slocum held the whip hand if he walked out of the cabin. Innick had no sway over him. Slocum was suddenly glad he had demanded cash rather than a check, which could have been voided in a heartbeat.

"That ruby's the most important thing in the world to my wife," Innick said. "It's been in her family for generations. She says that the King of France gave it to her great-great-grandmother. I think that's bullshit but she believes it."

Slocum waited. Innick worked himself up into asking for something more. When it came, Slocum found himself again indecisive about what to do.

"Get the ruby back, and I'll give you another five hundred."

The sum was too large to ignore. But his gut told him to have nothing more to do with the sawmill owner and his wife.

Still, another five hundred was like putting an open honey jar in front of a grizzly.

"In gold," Slocum said. "The reward has to be in gold." He pressed his hand against the bankroll in his coat pocket. Doubling that would be impressive, but he didn't trust paper money, not after the Panic of '72 and subsequent bank failures. Even greenbacks were suspect. He had seen men trading federal notes at a discount for flour and beans because no one believed they were worth the face amount.

Innick started to protest. His face got redder until Slocum thought he would explode. Then Innick said, "Very well."

The sudden agreement took Slocum by surprise. He had hoped Innick would deny the new condition on recovering the gemstone and let him off the hook.

"I'd better get to it. The longer I stand here, the harder it'll be to find that ruby."

Innick made shooing motions with both hands, then collapsed into his chair. Slocum had seen defeated men before—and he did now.

As he stepped out of the cabin, the spring air seemed a bit chillier than it should have. His mood lightened as he realized he was still in the driver's box. If he found the ruby, he could claim the reward. If he didn't find it, he could ride on and never return. Slocum patted the five hundred dollars already in his pocket and vowed to add that much more in gold.

"Let me talk to him," Slocum said to Marshal Smith. The corpulent man shifted his weight in the chair, causing both back legs to wobble.

"Now why'd I go and do that, Slocum? You still workin' for that son of a bitch Innick?"

"That doesn't have anything to do with me talking to the prisoner. He have a lawyer?"

"Hell, no. Who'd represent him? You took everything he had to pay a shyster. You give it all back to Innick?"

"I want to talk to him, Marshal. What's your objection?"

"You ain't an attorney, and I'm holdin' him *incognito* 'til the trial." The marshal rolled the word around on his tongue as if it were a fine whiskey. It might have been the only big word he knew—or thought he did.

Slocum looked into the back. The robber hung on the iron bars, listening to everything Slocum and the marshal said. It wouldn't take but an instant to call out to him. What would the marshal do? He couldn't even get to his feet fast enough to stop Slocum if he walked into the cell block.

But Slocum said nothing more, turned, and left the marshal huffing and puffing behind him. He looked around, then went to the side of the jailhouse and waited. After a decent pause, Marshal Smith came out, hitched up his gun belt, and made a beeline for the saloon across the street. Knowing Smith was likely smarter than he looked, Slocum waited. In less than a minute after pushing through the swinging doors at the saloon, the marshal came bustling back, opened the front door, and stuck his head in. Satisfied Slocum hadn't returned behind his back, Smith left again.

Rather than chance the lawman seeing him enter the jailhouse and accusing him of trying to talk to the prisoner, Slocum went around to the rear, found a crate, and pushed it under the barred window. Climbing up, he had a good look down into the cell where the prisoner sat disconsolate on the bunk.

"Not everything you stole was in the pouch," Slocum said. The prisoner jumped as if he had poked him with a toad sticker.

"You! What happened? Didn't that old skinflint pay you?"

"A ruby was missing."

"That a big red stone?"

"You know it is. Where is it? If I get it back, I'll see that you get out of this cell."

"You'd bust me out? The ruby's that important?"

"I'll even see that you have a horse. After that, you're on your own."

"Smith'd never bestir his carcass to come after me if I

get out of here," the thief said. He stood and peered out at Slocum. "I can't trust you. If I tell you where the ruby went, you'll leave me to rot."

"My word. Tell me what you did with the ruby, and I'll break you out."

The thief studied Slocum's face for a full minute, then said slowly, "Damned if I don't believe you. But you got to know the risk I'm takin'."

"I'll do as I promised."

"Ain't no love 'tween Innick and the marshal, that's for sure. I listen real good and know that's a fact. And you and the marshal don't get on too good either."

"I couldn't care less about the marshal or Innick. I'm being paid to do a job. If breaking you out is part of doing what I'm paid for, so be it."

"There was this fellow. He was the one who put me up to the robbery in the first place. He was dressed like he was from a circus."

Slocum remembered the storekeeper's description. Purple velvet coat, brocade vest, silk pants. That was close to the robber's description.

"Only he wasn't from a circus," Slocum said. "You said he told you about the jewelry?"

"He had it all planned out. A real thinker, he was. I did like he told me, and I waltzed away with everything. And that was the strange part."

"What?"

"He only wanted that ruby. The rest he let me keep. Seemed real happy with the ruby, too. He ran his finger over it like he was fondlin' a whore's tit. Couldn't have looked more satisfied if he had been, too."

The jailhouse outer door creaked open. Slocum caught a glimpse of the marshal and dropped out of sight.

"You promised!" the thief called.

And Slocum had. First he wanted to be sure about this peacock of a criminal mastermind.

* * *

Slocum laid another five-dollar bill on the counter as he said, "Sure do have some mighty fine supplies here."

The storekeeper licked his lips, looked from Slocum to the money and back when Slocum laid a ten-dollar bill down.

"You needin' supplies to get you all the way to Montana? That's plenty for that. Got some good bacon, too."

Slocum laid another five on the pile and waited.

"Can't tell you more 'n I already did," the man said. He rubbed his hands across his apron, leaving damp spots showing how nervous he was looking at so much money piled in front of him.

"A real dandy, you said."

"Never seen a man dressed like that before. Especially when I overheard how he wanted a carpenter." The storekeeper blinked. "Didn't remember he'd say nuthin' 'bout goin' to see Dillingham. Reckon that's because it was a week back and all I was thinkin' on was yesterday."

"This Dillingham have a shop in town?"

"Carpenter shop right down the road, you passed it comin' into town. Dill, he gets all his supplies from Mr. Innick. Danged good carpenter. Don't know why I hadn't remembered that before." He looked again at the pile of money.

"Have my supplies ready. I need to see a carpenter about a man gussied up like a peacock."

The stack of bills disappeared as if by magic before Slocum turned away. He thought the storekeeper had been honest enough and hadn't remembered, but money had a way of greasing the memory. But what could a man intent on stealing a ruby from Mrs. Innick want with a carpenter? Slocum set out to discover the reason.

Dillingham was in his shop, planing a long, rough board until it gleamed like a piece of polished metal. He was a youngish man, thick of chest with immensely powerful arms. Slocum vowed to avoid getting into a fight with the carpenter, and if he did, an ax handle across the top of his shaved head would be the first tactic.

"Evening," Dillingham greeted Slocum, putting down the plane and wiping his hands on a rag. "You work for Innick, don't you?"

"On the saw until yesterday," Slocum said. He laid out his question, deciding this wasn't a man who fancied himself to be much of a talker and wouldn't mince words.

Dillingham stroked his clean-shaven chin, then worked to brush sawdust from his bushy mustache. He finally said, "I did some work for this gent."

"I need to talk to him. Might be I could deliver some of the work for you, if you could tell me where to find him."

"He put in the order a week back. Wagon pulled up yesterday, and me and him loaded the crates. Six of 'em. For a fellow so purty dressed, he managed to hold his own." Dillingham laughed and shook his head. "Can't see how he did it but didn't get so much as a spot on them duds of his."

"Crates?"

"Had me make him six crates about yea long and this high. Only two feet thick but with spacers inside. He was determined that the spacers be nailed down, not glued, though that'd have been easier. Said something about glue melting. No idea what he was worryin' about."

Slocum estimated the crates were four feet long, three high, and two feet thick with a half dozen of the thin spacers inside making parallel channels.

"You have any idea what he was going to do with the crates?"

"Never asked. He paid good. Turned out to be easier than I thought since I could cut most of the sides at the same time. Then I . . ."

Slocum let the man go on about his expertise. He looked outside and saw that the sun had dipped down. The air would be turning cold.

"You see which way he went with the wagon? He was driving, wasn't he?"

"He was, too, and doin' a fair job of that. He might be decked out as a dandy but he was mighty skilled. Even said he would have made the crates himself but there wasn't time. Drove off in a hurry."

"North?"

"You know this gent? Likely he was headin' for Sage Creek Junction since there's not a whole lot else thataway. You tell him I'll be glad to make more of them crates any-time he wants. Paid good."

Slocum left the carpenter's shop, the sound of the wood plane sliding over the plank fading as he walked down the main street toward the jailhouse. He had learned about all he could.

It was time to keep his promise and break a sneak thief out of the calaboose.

4

Slocum watched the jailhouse door carefully for any sign that Marshal Smith was moving about inside. When it opened and the portly lawman came waddling out, Slocum slid back into the shadows, waiting to see what would happen. As earlier, the marshal walked across the street, went into the saloon, probably knocked back a quick beer, and came out to be sure the jail was undisturbed. Knowing the routine, Slocum hadn't moved a muscle.

This time the marshal didn't return to the jailhouse but went farther down the street to a restaurant and went in. Considering the man's girth, he was likely going to be a while. Slocum walked quickly to the door, pulled up on the latch, and slid inside.

"You came for me! I thought you was lyin'!"

Slocum made a sour face. That was the same as calling him a liar, but if their positions had been swapped, he wasn't sure if he wouldn't harbor the same suspicions.

"What you said about the dandy was true." Slocum rummaged through the desk hunting for the keys to the cell.

"He takes the keys with him," the prisoner called. "You're gonna have to shoot off the lock."

"Like hell. He's only a few yards down the street. Any commotion would bring him running," Slocum said.

The prisoner laughed.

"At top speed, that'd still give better 'n an hour to get free."

Slocum knew he joked. He had nothing to back up his suspicion, but he guessed Marshal Smith had a mean streak a mile wide. He was more likely to kill an escaping prisoner than recapture him. That was tidier and didn't take near as much effort.

Slocum went to the cell and examined the lock, then looked up.

"Can you jimmy it open if I get something to pick the lock?"

"I ain't that kind of thief." To emphasize the point, he rattled the bars.

Slocum stepped back, saw how sturdy the jail was in spite of the slovenly marshal, and shook his head. For an instant he considered blasting off the lock, but he'd never had much luck doing that with any but padlocks that swung free on cash boxes. More likely, the lead would spatter throughout the lock and make it impossible to ever open.

"Don't go anywhere," Slocum said.

"Wait, you can't leave me!"

Slocum slipped back through the door, saw that the marshal had taken a table in the front window of the restaurant and worked furiously to shovel in food. Every now and then he'd glance up to be sure his jail was intact, then he'd return to devouring his meal.

Slocum got his horse and another he had bought for the robber. Leading them around to the rear, he got back up on the crate and slipped a rope around the bars in the window.

"When I yank 'em free, you get on out."

"I don't know if I can jump that high."

"That's your problem. There's a horse waiting for you on

this side of the wall." Slocum looped the other end of the rope around the saddle horn on the robber's horse and got it pulling.

The horse strained, balked. Slocum kept it pulling hard. Then he heard a tearing sound as the bars ripped free of the masonry wall. When the horse surged forward, he had to make a wild grab to keep it from running off. The bars crashed to the ground with a sound loud enough to wake the dead. He paused, every sense alert. How the marshal could have missed such a racket was beyond him, unless that restaurant served up a mighty mean peach cobbler for dessert.

The next sound he heard was a boot scrabbling against a rock wall. The robber's arms came through the window, then his head and shoulders. He flopped about, belly over the ledge, feet in and torso out. With a mighty heave, he fell out, landing on his head. He sat up, rubbing his temple.

Slocum rode back and tossed him the reins to the horse.

"There's some vittles in the saddlebags, too. I don't advise you stopping to eat, though, until you're a good long ways off."

"Much obliged." The robber swung into the saddle and turned the horse's face northward.

"Not that way," Slocum said. "Any way but north."

"Why not?"

"You don't want to ride with me." Slocum rested his hand on the ebony handle of his Colt.

The robber's head bobbed up and down like it was on a spring, then he galloped off westward. That direction suited Slocum since the wagon with the specially made crates had gone north. He wasted no time getting on the trail himself. Marshal Smith wasn't going to take kindly to losing a prisoner—or anyone who had helped the prisoner escape.

He rode slowly through the night along the double-rutted road, figuring a man driving a wagon wasn't likely to veer off anytime soon. This seemed especially true since the dandy driving the wagon with the crates wasn't from these parts. The carpenter had no idea what the crates were for, yet the man ordering them had precise dimensions and requirements. The clerk at the mercantile likely knew everyone within a twenty-mile radius of town, and he hadn't seen the dandy prior to a week earlier.

As Slocum trotted along, the morning sun poking up over the trees, he considered that the man he sought had come up from Salt Lake City. The lure of the Innick jewels might have attracted him, but Slocum thought it was more likely he had spotted Mrs. Innick wearing the fancy pendant with the ruby inset. But why hadn't he kept more of the loot? A generous thief was a contradiction Slocum couldn't wrap his head around. If the dandy planned the robbery, he should have taken more than the single ruby as his due. Instead he had given the rest of the valuable loot to the robber now likely halfway across the Wasatch Mountains.

A crime of convenience? Of circumstance? Why did the robber want the crates and only the ruby? Slocum wondered if this crook knew the Innick family and had a special animus toward them. Mrs. Innick had said the ruby was a wedding present for her daughter. Robbing her of that gift might hurt her more than stealing the rest of the jewelry. Slocum even wondered if the gussied-up thief wasn't inclined to taunt the family that he possessed what they no longer had.

He glanced over his shoulder, estimating where the sawmill was to the east and south. It would take him a day at most to return and find out if a ransom had been requested for the stolen gem. Then he looked at the weeds alongside the road and saw how they had been crushed down recently by a heavy wagon traveling north. The thief had kept the stone.

"Five hundred dollars," Slocum repeated over and over. He had spent close to a hundred of the first part of his reward on horses, gear, and supplies, not to mention a bribe to grease the storekeeper's memory, but it had been worth it.

Not only was he on the ruby thief's trail, but he had supplies enough to last weeks so he wouldn't have to take time to hunt. It would be only a matter of time before he overtook the wagon, recovered the stolen ruby—and got some answers. If anything, he was as anxious to find out what this was all about as he was to return the ruby to Innick for the next five-hundred-dollar reward.

In gold.

By late in the day he passed riders going southward. He hailed them and asked, "What's ahead?"

"Town, not a mile farther," came the answer.

"You seen a man driving a wagon?" It irked Slocum that he got a loud laugh in response. "Well, have you?"

"Mister, wagons is 'bout all we've seen these past two weeks."

Before he could ask, the riders rode on. He considered going after them and finding what that cryptic answer meant, then realized a better way to find what he wanted to know lay a mile on up the road. A trot brought him to the town within fifteen minutes.

The town sat in a bowl at the edge of the mountains. He wasn't sure but thought he had crossed over into Wyoming, and these mountains were part of the Tetons. From experience, he estimated a small town like Sage Creek Junction boasted no more than two hundred residents. He hunted for the wagons the riders had mentioned but saw nothing out of the ordinary. Not sure if they had been making fun of a stranger, he rode down the center of the main street.

This might have been any of a hundred towns he had seen while drifting throughout the West. It was large enough for three saloons but not so big that it needed more than a solitary bank. A telegraph line ran toward the southwest, possibly linking the town with Logan or even Salt Lake City.

He dismounted, secured the reins, and went into a saloon. On a small stage two skinny girls danced, flouncing their skirts up high enough to be daring but not so high as to expose anything worthwhile. The piano clinked out a tune Slocum could—almost—recognize. But what did draw him was the promise of a beer and a free beef sandwich.

"You got the look of a man in serious need of wetting his whistle," the barkeep said. The man was short and, as he moved, limped just a mite. His hands never slowed from restless movement, as if he was slowly shaking himself to death.

"Food, beer, those are what I'm in need of." Slocum placed a five-dollar bill on the bar. As the barkeep reached for it, Slocum kept it pinned with his trigger finger. "And some information."

"The first two you can pay for. The gossip's free, if it's about local folks. But secrets? Ain't for sale at any price. I got to live in this town."

"Fair enough," Slocum said, taking change from for the scrip and starting to work on a sandwich filled with tough meat and a smear of mustard. He washed down chunks of it with beer and then ordered another. When the bartender slid it to him, Slocum said, "I'm not much for gossip, but two gents riding out of town said there were a passel of wagons here. Don't see them anywhere."

"That's what you wanted to know about? Hell, mister, just ask anybody. Them folks spread money around like there was no tomorrow. We was all sorry to see them leave."

"When?"

"This morning, with the cock's crow. Twenty-four wagons. I know since I counted 'em as they rolled out."

"One loaded with new crates?"

"Hell, all of 'em was loaded down with crates and equipment. It was a gov'mint mapping expedition, headin' toward Yellowstone."

"There a jeweler in town? Somebody who deals in jewelry?"

"Got a fellow from Germany what repairs watches. You mean something like that?"

"Reckon so." Slocum finished his beer and sandwich, got

directions to the watchmaker, and made his way through the almost deserted town to the shop.

The sounds of cuckoo clocks signaling the hour greeted him as he went inside. A man with a magnifying eyepiece mounted on a pair of spectacles looked up. For an instant his eye looked ten times its real size. Then he took out the magnifying piece and asked, "What is it I can do for you, sir? A fine pocket watch? Repair?"

"You buy jewels?"

"That is an odd question, but I do."

"You buy a ruby recently?"

"What is the purpose of this questioning?" The watchmaker, a stocky man with muttonchops and thick hands at odds with the fine work he performed on the watch spread out on his worktable, stood. He reached for a rag on the side of the table.

"No need to get all het up," Slocum said. The outline of a small pistol under the rag hinted at gunplay if he didn't calm the man fast. "I'm looking for a man who might have sold you a ruby."

"A ruby? Pah!" The watchmaker pressed his hand down near the rag hiding the pistol but made no further move to grab for the weapon. "I buy hundreds of gemstones. Rubies are best for my mechanisms."

"You use rubies in a watch?" Slocum frowned.

"At friction points, yes. It reduces wear, does away with need for constant oiling, makes the watch last tens of years rather than one or two. Metal on metal wears out too soon."

"The ruby I mean would be about this big." Slocum put thumb and forefinger into a circle to indicate the size of the stone removed from Mrs. Innick's pendant.

"My rubies are this big!" The watchmaker pressed his thumbnail against his pinky finger. "Smaller! They are no more than the head of a pin. See?" He lifted a small glass jar and rattled it. The light reflected off dozens of red specks so small Slocum almost missed them.

"You have any need for a ruby as big as the one I'm look-ing for?"

"Not even that horrific Big Ben in London uses such. The English horologists needed good Teutonic advice to build such a mechanism, but they chose Denison and Airy. Pah!" The watchmaker made a dismissive gesture.

Slocum had no idea what he meant.

"Did a dandy offer you a ruby for sale?"

The man shook his head, then shrugged.

"I have no use for such things. My wares are available for any to see." He made a sweeping gesture taking in the small shop.

Slocum glanced around. The man sold watch chains but no other gold jewelry.

"You talk to any of them in the mapping expedition?"

"I did," the man said. "The leader, Dr. Hayden, appreci-ated my work and bought five fine timepieces. He said they were to be used in the mapping."

Slocum turned the name over in his head, but he had never heard of anyone named Hayden. That meant nothing, but he knew who to ask after now. He thanked the watch-maker and stepped out into the street. If he rode hard, he could overtake the expedition before sundown.

The warm sun on his back cast a long shadow in front of Slo-cum as he rode slowly toward the mountain meadow where the large expedition had camped for the night. As he approached the wagons, he did a quick count. Twenty-four. The barkeep knew his arithmetic.

More than counting the wagons, he hunted for one loaded with the crates Dillingham had built. Most of the beds were still hidden by tarps. The few that exposed their contents car-ried food for the expedition. A chuck wagon at the far side of the meadow had a sizable number of men gathered, while oth-ers lugged parcels from the wagons for the cook to use in pre-paring the meal for what must have been several dozen men.

He reached the last of the wagons before anyone hailed him. A man dressed in a prissy suit that was too small for him and a bowler hat that perched atop his head like the knob on a mushroom stepped forward. He held a rifle in the crook of his left arm but didn't seem too anxious that a stranger entered his camp.

"Howdy, you with the expedition?"

"Just riding past and saw you camped here," Slocum answered. "This the Yellowstone mapping expedition I heard about?"

"Sure is. You fixin' to join up? You got the look of a scout. We got two already but kin always use another, I reckon."

"Not sure. Where can I find Hayden?" Slocum's question put the sentry at ease. The watchmaker had remembered the leader's name for Slocum to use.

"Chowin' down, I reckon. Go on over. Might be you can get a plate of beans, too."

"Sounds like just the thing to finish off the day's ride," Slocum said. He touched the brim of his hat and rode slowly, taking a meandering course through the wagons. He saw nothing that matched the description of Dillingham's crates.

Try as he might, Slocum couldn't figure out what those crates would be used for on a mapping expedition, yet the trail led directly to this meadow and these men. As he dismounted a few yards from the chuck wagon, he began searching among the men for the dandy in the purple velvet coat and silk trousers. While many were strangely dressed, like the sentry, he saw no one that stood out in purple and gold.

"I don't recognize you, sir. I am Dr. Ferdinand Hayden, leader of this expedition." He canted his head to one side as he studied Slocum, then added, "We are authorized by the government of the United States."

That held no particular cachet for Slocum.

"I saw your camp and thought I'd stop by. Looks like a big expedition."

"Mapping, sir. We are fifty strong."

"Good work," Slocum said, nodding.

"Have you ever been part of such an expedition?"

"Done some surveying in my day," Slocum allowed, "but I'm more comfortable scouting." He cursed the words that slid from his lips when he saw how Hayden brightened.

"We are in sore need of another good scout. Are you familiar with this area? The indigenous natives?"

"The Indians?" Slocum sucked at his teeth and thought hard. "Haven't heard of any trouble brewing with the Crow or Arapaho. Don't reckon you'll have problems on that score."

"Our third scout found himself in jail. Drunkenness is not to be countenanced in this party."

Slocum wanted to ask about the crates the carpenter had made but saw no easy way to pose the question and seem other than a drifter passing by.

"Can understand that. You don't want to map the same terrain over and over," Slocum said. Hayden did not take it as the joke Slocum had intended.

"You are welcome to share our evening meal, sir."

The implication was that Slocum had to leave immediately after. He wanted to look under more of the tarps hiding so many of the wagon beds' cargo, but it might be better if he did ride away, then return to prowl around when the camp bedded down for the night. He doubted Hayden would post adequate guards, not the first night on the trail.

"Much obliged." Slocum saw the others in the party had already helped themselves to a savory stew. He let the cook dish out a full ladle on a tin plate for him, then toss on a couple biscuits.

The cook said nothing. Slocum was about to thank him when he saw movement—slow, sinuous, and utterly feminine. He half turned and slopped some stew onto his fingers, burning them. Slocum paid no attention. The woman hurried between two wagons, on her way toward an enclosed wagon. Slender, brunette, every move a thing of grace and beauty, she kept her face hidden from Slocum until the last moment when she went up the two steps to the enclosed wagon and opened the door. In that instant Slocum got a good look at her.

An angel might have come to earth. Then she disappeared into the wagon.

Slocum started to ask after her, even knowing he wasn't likely to get any decent response. A woman that lovely had to be in the dreams—and care—of every man in the expedition.

A wagon rattled past, the tarp flapping in the evening breeze. While Slocum couldn't be sure, the cargo might well have been the crates Dillingham had built. Then the driver, wearing a heavy duster, yee-hawed, snapped the reins smartly, got the team pulling in a different direction, and disappeared behind a line of other wagons.

In the dark, Slocum couldn't be sure, but poking out from under the sleeve of the canvas duster might have been a flash of white lace cuff—and bright purple coat sleeve.

He gobbled down the stew, cleaned off the plate, then said to Hayden, "Thanks for the hospitality."

"May your trip be a safe one," the expedition leader said.

With any luck, Slocum could recover the ruby this very night and return to Innick's sawmill in three or four days. He was on his way to earning another five hundred dollars.

5

Slocum had been wrong. Hayden had posted guards, and being on the trail for such a short time, they were eager and alertly patrolled their stations. Flat on his belly, he studied the guard nearest him. It was the man in the tight-fitting suit he had encountered riding into the camp. The man tried to present a military demeanor, actually marching to and fro with his rifle hiked up on his shoulder, but such playacting wore on him after an hour.

Not knowing when the sentry would be relieved, Slocum had to make the effort to look in the wagons. The guard finally sat on a rock and pulled off a shoe to rub his tender foot. Slocum had guessed right that this wasn't a man used to either patrolling or walking.

As the man made soft moaning sounds while he worked on his aching toes, Slocum began his search. He rose and walked on cat's feet, passing within a dozen feet of the man without alerting him. With a quick few steps, he ended up under the nearest wagon. Slocum knew he had to be careful because the expedition had pitched their bedrolls near their wagons.

He almost stepped on one snoring man as he slipped underneath and came out on the far side. Slocum stood, decided boldness was his ally, and began walking about as if he belonged in the camp. The guards had all been watching for intruders from the outside. No one questioned a man moving around within the camp. It took him the better part of an hour before he found the wagon with the specially constructed crates. Tugging back the edge of a dusty tarpaulin, he ran his fingers over the side of the nearest case.

Dillingham did good work. Slocum found no trace of roughness, and the insides had been especially well finished. Slocum drew his fingers over what might have been a highly polished decorative bowl for all the skill lavished on it. Fragrant wood made his nostrils flare. But the slots within the cases were all empty.

The crunch of boots against gravel caused him to hop into the wagon and pull the tarp down enough so he could peer out. Not five feet away stood a tall thin man. Slocum started to scoot forward to get a closer look when he heard someone else approaching.

"Ah, good evening, Dr. Hayden," the man greeted. "Such a fine night out in the wilderness."

"We have yet to reach the wilderness, sir," Hayden said. "I want a more complete record on this expedition than that of any previous one. Yellowstone must be presented in its full glory to Congress. I am especially certain we can convince them to make this a national park."

"I agree. My artistry will have them gasping for breath, begging for mercy, falling over themselves to preserve the subject of my paintings," the man said, striking a pose, one hand over his heart and the other reaching for the heavens. "I do say, those stars are larger out here. More brilliant."

"Can you paint by starlight?"

"Hardly. Nor can I photograph at night. My skills require the full force of sunlight to bring out detail, not obscure it in penumbra."

"When you are ready, head out and . . ."

The rest of Hayden's words faded as the two men turned their backs to Slocum and walked away. Slocum scrambled forward and peered out. He thought he identified the pair as they zigzagged through camp, then could not be sure. Their discussion had caused several sleeping nearby to mumble and groan, restlessly turning over. Taking a few more seconds to assure himself these were the crates he sought that would lead him to the ruby thief, Slocum dropped to the ground and made his way back out of camp. The man hadn't been the popinjay from back in Otter Creek, but more than one person on the expedition could have been involved in the ruby's theft. The man had come straight for the wagon holding the custom-made cases and had reached out, as if to check them. Only Hayden had interrupted the examination.

Slocum was so deep in thought, he grew careless.

"Halt!"

Slocum's hand flew to his six-shooter, then he froze. Shooting a guard would only bring the rest of the camp down on his head. He faced the man in the ill-fitting suit. He had slipped back into his shoe but hobbled a mite as he stepped toward Slocum, the rifle swinging about.

"Be careful with that thing," Slocum said in a husky whisper. "I'm here to relieve you."

"Dr. Hayden told me I'd be out here for another hour."

"Then go back to patrolling. I can use the sleep," Slocum said, coughing to cover his voice even more.

"No, wait. If the doctor told you to come out, then I must have gotten the times wrong."

"Go on, get some sleep," Slocum said. He had to turn his face away as the man handed over the rifle. "You lucky son of a bitch."

That produced a genuine laugh and sealed the deal.

The would-be guard hobbled off, chuckling at his good fortune. Slocum quietly retrieved his horse, rode away from the camp about fifty yards, found a stump and rested the rifle against it, then faded into the darkness. The derelict guard might be chewed out for deserting his post, but Slocum doubted it. If someone found the rifle, he would consider himself lucky and never figure out what had happened since nothing would be missing from camp.

Slocum rode back into the camp as they were hitching the teams and preparing to head northward. He waved to the man he had relieved of guard duty the night before, then trotted to the head of the line, where Ferdinand Hayden sat astride a powerful black stallion. To Slocum's surprise, the man's seat looked secure and he seemed in full control of the spirited horse.

"You're back," Hayden said in a neutral tone.

"I am. You mentioned a job as a scout. I've got some experience and nothing better to do. Since I'm heading north, too, I might as well get paid for it."

Hayden stared hard at Slocum, then said, "You were a Rebel, weren't you?"

"I was. And you were a Federal. From the look, you're a medical doctor."

"I patched up my share of the wounded during the war," Hayden said. "I saw more than my share die from Southern bullets."

"The war's over." Slocum tried to place the man's accent. Likely Massachusetts, and if it wasn't his home, Slocum knew he wasn't off by much.

"It is, sir, it is. Well over. What is your experience?"

Slocum told of a few parties he had scouted for. Hayden's expression never changed, but one of them must have hit the mark because he finally pursed his lips, then nodded.

"You're hired. Five dollars a week, grub, and privileges."

"What might those privileges be?" Slocum asked in surprise.

Hayden grinned.

"Why, no one's ever asked. I don't rightly know. The

people in this expedition are all so dedicated to mapping the Yellowstone, they might have paid for the chance to accompany me rather than I paying them."

"What's the first thing you need? The road's pretty much blazed. From the look of traffic, it'll be a few more days before we run out of it."

"Ride along, get a feel for the company. You're with scientists intent on their studies. My other two scouts lit out at dawn. I have no idea where they are or I'd advise you to get acquainted with them also."

Slocum had figured that out from everything Hayden said. Mostly Northerners, mostly stolen away from universities and government agencies in Washington. From the way the expedition leader talked of the other scouts, he wasn't satisfied with their skill.

"What's that wagon?" Slocum pointed to the tall, enclosed wagon he had seen the lovely woman enter the night before. "Looks like a wagon more at home in a gypsy caravan."

"Ah, the Romany," Hayden said. "That's a rolling darkroom. We have a fine photographer with us to capture the exact details of the land. William Henry Jackson is both a painter and a photographer. You might have heard of him."

"Can't say I have."

"He is as famous as Mathew Brady."

"Him, I've heard of," Slocum said. "He in the expedition, too?"

"Hardly. Dealing with Mr. Jackson's temperament is difficulty enough for me without adding to the mix. At times I think William is more artist than photographer, though there is considerable artistry involved in what he does. He plans to do large-sized photographs."

Slocum heard the gurgling of liquids in the wagon. He knew a little of the process used by photographers. Once the glass plate was exposed, it was dipped in a variety of noxious chemicals until a negative appeared. From this a print could be made. That all the equipment necessary resided in the wagon was nothing less than a marvel.

"Be sure to introduce yourself to those in the party." Hayden put his heels to his stallion's flanks and rocketed away to speak with a man struggling to control his team, giving advice and pointing out that the driver should avoid the larger rocks in the road.

Slocum trotted forward and came even with the driver of the photographic wagon. A slow smile came to his lips.

"Good morning, ma'am," he said, touching the brim of his Stetson. The woman expertly handled the team.

"Why, good morning, sir. Do I know you?"

Slocum introduced himself.

"I am Marlene Wilkes."

"Pleased to make your acquaintance, Miss Wilkes. You do more than drive this wagon?"

"I am Mr. Jackson's assistant, though he does not openly acknowledge me as such."

"You take photographs?" Seeing her eyebrows arch in surprise, Slocum explained that Hayden had told him the nature of the wagon.

"I am sure he was quite precise. That is his way. That makes him an excellent cartographer."

"He had nice things to say about your employer, too. Not only a photographer but an artist."

"Quite a famous one," Marlene said.

Slocum sat a little straighter as an idea hit him.

"How does he carry the finished paintings?"

He barely listened as Marlene explained how special crates had been built for this purpose. She described the cases Dillingham had built to a tee.

"Where is he?"

"Oh, you mean to ask why he isn't driving? That you imply that's a chore not fit for a woman?"

Slocum smiled crookedly and said, "I've seen women muleskinners who were tougher than men with their teams."

"Are you implying I am one of these women . . . tough muleskinners?"

"I haven't been around long enough to know what you're good at—other than handling this team."

"William is ahead doing sketches," she said, her smile matching Slocum's. "We shall be stopping soon for the noon meal."

"Ahead, you say?"

"If I know him, he will be sketching those mountains yonder. They have a certain majesty to them that would undoubtedly appeal to him."

"They call this range the Grand Tetons." Slocum squinted a bit. "Because they look like a woman's tits from far enough away."

"Sir! I am outraged!"

Slocum laughed and galloped away. Marlene sounded anything but outraged, and the look of the mountains made it hard to describe them in any other fashion. His good humor faded as he rode ahead, on the lookout for fresh tracks. It took him only a few minutes to see the shod hoofprints. Since it had rained the night before, these had to be recent. And being shod, the tracks didn't belong to an Indian pony. When the tracks veered away from the main road, Slocum followed.

A mile off the road he came to rolling meadow, fresh and green and fragrant with an explosion of flowers in its spring glory. But even Slocum could appreciate the beauty of the mountains as seen from here. Not a half mile across the meadow he saw a small figure moving about restlessly. Slocum shielded his eyes and made out an easel all set up. The artist moved across the dull white canvas often enough for him to get a decent look at the man.

This had to be William Jackson.

Slocum rode slowly to avoid spooking the man, but from the amount of concentration he put into his work, nothing short of a gunshot would pull him away. Slocum guessed that even this might not be enough unless he put the slug into the man's arm and forced him to drop his paintbrush.

The artist worked quickly. In the time it took Slocum to cover the distance between them, most of the scene had been sketched in. Jackson worked with quick, sure strokes, hardly paying any attention to the palette but shifting his gaze back and forth between the mountain scenery and his canvas.

"Mighty fine drawing," Slocum said.

Jackson turned, glared, then returned to work without a word.

"You been with the Hayden expedition all the way from Salt Lake City?"

"Sir," the artist said, not bothering to turn, "I am working. Whoever you are and whatever you think you're doing, leave me be. I have little time."

"What's the hurry?" Slocum dismounted, eased the leather thong off the Colt's hammer, and moved around to see the man's hands. If he dropped the paintbrush or palette and went for a gun, Slocum was ready to throw down on him. Marlene Wilkes had said it had been Jackson who'd ordered the special cases made. The dandy with his purple coat and silk britches must be nothing more than another assistant.

"The light, sir, the light! And that damnable Hayden you mentioned has his own purpose, and it is not to capture the beauty of the land. He wants to turn this—*this*—into nothing more than connected lines on a sheet of paper. A topographical map has no beauty, no sense of nature. Now leave me alone."

"You hear about a robbery from Sean Innick?"

"I have never heard of this man. What is he to me?" Jackson turned and faced Slocum squarely. "More to the point, what is he to you that you continue to annoy me? Has this Innick sent you to be my person from Porlock? Are you to interrupt greatness and deny the world a glimpse of true beauty?"

"Innick's wife had her jewelry stolen," Slocum said, studying the man closely. "I retrieved most of it, all save a ruby. That's a red gemstone."

"I know what a ruby is, dolt!"

"You hire a thief to steal it?"

"You are both annoying and insulting! Go away. Do you work for Hayden? I must have words with him about the low quality of his employees. I told him not to hire local ruffians."

"Marshal Smith might have questions for you about the theft," Slocum said. His hand moved to the butt of his six-shooter.

"I don't know this Smith, Innick, or *you*. Now leave or I shall have to thrash you." Jackson put down his brush and palette and stepped toward Slocum.

The artist didn't look like a barroom brawler. Slocum considered whether to throw down and put an end to this or maybe trade a few punches. He knew he would prevail, and hitting the man a few times would loosen his tongue about stealing the ruby.

As Jackson moved, he skinned out of his white smock. Beneath it he wore a dull brown coat with matching trousers, a plaid vest, and a dingy shirt that poked out at the collar.

"You have special cases made up for your paintings?" Slocum asked.

Jackson stopped in his tracks and stared.

"You are a peculiar man. Of course I have carrying cases for my work."

This satisfied Slocum that he could drag the artist back to Otter Creek and let the marshal deal with him. The ruby had to be in the man's belongings, perhaps hidden in that fancy darkroom wagon. Slocum rested his hand on his pistol when he hard a loud cry.

"Mr. Jackson! Dr. Hayden wants to see you immediately."

Slocum chanced a quick look over his shoulder. Marlene Wilkes rode toward them, waving. Slocum didn't know if she waved to him or to draw her employer's attention. Whichever it was, he did not draw. Taking Jackson into custody would require considerable explanation he wasn't up to making in front of the woman. She obviously thought the world of William Jackson.

"Oh, bother," Jackson said, lowering his balled fists. He picked up his white smock and tossed it back over a case. By now Marlene had ridden up and sat astride her horse only a few yards away. "Do pack up all this, will you, Miss Wilkes? How can a man get any work done with all these interruptions?" He glared at Slocum, spun, and stalked to his horse.

With an easy grace, he mounted and trotted off, leaving Slocum to wonder how he was going to find the ruby.

"You really shouldn't bother him when he is working, Mr. Slocum. When he gets into one of his snits, he is quite impossible for hours and hours." She dropped to the ground and went to the easel. "He is truly a remarkable artist." She looked from the sketch to the subject and back. "A genius with the brush as well as the camera."

"What did Hayden want to talk to him about?"

"Oh, I don't know. Well, I do. Nothing. I lied. Dr. Hayden said nothing to me about talking with William. By the time they find one another, something will have come up, though. It always does."

"You sent him on a wild-goose chase?"

"Yes," she said, turning her limpid brown eyes on him. "Why?"

"How else could we be alone for a while?" She took a step toward him, then stopped.

"Why would you want to be alone with me?"

She shrugged, then smiled wickedly.

"It is a beautiful day, and you are a beautiful man. Unless I am completely wrong, you similarly find me—"

"Beautiful," Slocum said, kissing her. Hard.

6

"I want you, John. Here. Now."

Slocum answered with actions rather than words. He kissed across her forehead and over closed eyes, those brown eyes that were so passionate and demanding. From here he silenced her for a moment with a kiss to her lips before moving lower, to a slender neck with a throbbing vein at the side that betrayed her arousal.

His lips pushed aside the neckline of her dress, exposing just enough of the surge of her breasts to excite him even more. The soft flesh flowed like silk under his lips, his tongue, his lustful gaze. Marlene reached up and tugged at her blouse, pulling the cloth down to expose even more of her luscious breasts. When a pink nipple popped free, Slocum pounced on it. His lips circled it. He sucked. Marlene gasped as she arched her back, trying to thrust more of her teat into his mouth.

He opened his mouth enough to take more of her. The soft flesh became his plaything. His tongue teased her nip, then pressed the hardening point back into the breast.

"That feels so nice, John, so good. But I want more."

Her fingers clawed at his back, curved into talons that

raked his flesh. This spurred him on. He ran his hands under her blouse, felt her heaving sides, and traced across every rib. He felt her frenzied heart accelerate even more as her passions rose. With a quick lift, he skinned her out of her blouse, leaving her naked to the waist. The warm sunlight bathed her twin glories rivaling the majestic stony peaks to the east, but these were warm and pliant and so much more inviting.

He kissed down one slope and licked upward in a slow, tormenting spiral to capture the hard nub cresting the other. She pressed closer to him. When he felt her legs buckle, he held her upright so she didn't collapse. Slowly lowering her to the ground, he found himself atop her. Marlene struggled under him, her legs spreading and her knees lifting on either side of his body.

Slocum struggled to get her skirts out of the way but found himself tangled.

"Wait, no, this way," she said. Her knees locked hard on his flanks then she heaved hard and rolled them over so Slocum was on the bottom and she reared above him, looking down.

Slocum liked this just fine. Her breasts bobbed as she rocked back, giving him a delightful view. The sun cast deep shadows between those warm peaks, giving her an exotic, exciting look. With a twitch of her hips, she lifted enough to reposition her skirts, then reached under them. At first Slocum thought she was tugging away her bloomers, then felt her quick fingers popping open the buttons on his fly.

He moaned in pleasure as she freed him and wrapped those agile fingers around his stiffening length. A few quick strokes made him steely hard and ready for what came next.

"I want this, John, I want you," she said in a sex-husky voice.

He reached up and cupped her breasts. The pressure of his palms against her nipples caused her to clamp her hands over his to push down even harder. She closed her eyes and tossed her head back to give voice to a loud cry of pure animal lust. When she began twisting side to side, her increasingly wet, warm privates rubbing against his manhood, Slocum reached the limits of his endurance.

"In," he said, pulling one hand away. He worked under her skirts and ran his fingers across her nether lips. The lady juices leaking from her insides lubricated his hand. He ran a finger into her, then began swirling it about. She went wild with need, rising, dropping, rocking, and twisting about. After the soft ruddy flush started on her white throat and spread downward to her tits, he knew she was ready for him.

Fumbling about, he positioned himself under those tender sex lips, then arched his back enough to sink an inch into her. It was as if all her strength fled. She collapsed, crashing downward and taking him balls deep.

"Oh," she said, "so big, so very big inside me."

Then her hips went berserk. She lifted and fell back repeatedly, speed increasing. Slocum felt her warmth all around, clutching at him, squeezing down as if she had gripped him wearing a velvet glove. He reached around her and cupped her buttocks, reveling in the feel of her muscles as she strained to move. As he squeezed down on the doughy mounds, she slammed down fully around him and cried out. Her body shook like a leaf in a high wind, and the blush spread even more fully across her breasts.

The shudders subsided and her eyes opened. Those brown eyes lacked the sharpness they had before. Now slightly unfocused by the power of her release, she blinked a few times. A tiny smile curled her lips as she said, "That was wonderful, John."

"Going to get even better," he said, straining to sit up. His arms circled her body and held her as he repositioned her.

His legs were stretched out while hers thrust straight on either side of his body. He split her wide open. Still buried in her, he began rocking back and forth. This moved him a little, but in ways that built enough friction against different portions of her heated tunnel.

"Th-That's like nothing I've ever f-felt," she gasped out. She buried her face in his shoulder as he continued to rock.

The movements were small. The effect was huge. He

hardened to the point where he thought he would go out of his mind with need. When she clamped down all around him, a warm and willing mine shaft collapsing on him, he jetted out his spunk. Slocum never stopped the slow, deliberate movement, and this added to his release. Marlene gasped as another climax seized her.

They sat face to face, her legs around him, for several minutes enjoying the muzzy afterglow. Marlene finally flopped back, resting on Slocum's legs. He tried not to look at her breasts and failed.

"Again?" she asked, using one hand to balance on the ground and the other to toy with her nipples.

"I'm not made out of stone," Slocum said.

"Could have fooled me. What I felt was long and hard as rock."

Slocum laughed. This had been unexpected and what he had been missing for so long. He put his hands on her waist and lifted so she could get her knees under her. From here she gracefully stood and stepped back to look down at his crotch.

"I can get it hard again. I'm quite the . . . stonemason."

"You certainly are," Slocum said, "but won't Hayden—or Jackson—be expecting you back at camp?"

"I do declare, Mr. Slocum, a girl might think you had no interest in her with talk like that." She bent over and lightly flicked the tip of his flaccid organ.

A small tingle passed down into his body. He pushed her hand away. As much as he wanted to see what more Marlene had in store for him, he wasn't up for it. Not for a while.

"Spoilsport," she said with a mock pout as he stood and started to button up. "If you're going to be like that, at least let me help." She dropped to her knees and took him in both hands, but she didn't push him back into his jeans that way. She used her tongue.

Slocum felt more than a little desire stirring, but by the time she had finished tucking him away and buttoning his fly, he knew the moment had passed. She looked up at him and smiled.

"That's so you have something to look forward to."

"Next time?"

"My, aren't you the presumptuous one, thinking there will be a 'next time'?"

"But you just said—"

Marlene laughed, and Slocum knew she was teasing him.

"I do need to pack all this away. Why don't you help me lash it onto my horse, then go off while I return to camp?"

Slocum understood. If they both returned after such a delay, Jackson might be suspicious of their activities. Dr. Hayden would certainly look askance at such goings-on. It could only cause ill feelings among the rest of the expedition.

Slocum had what they didn't. Or was Marlene the sort to work her way through the entire expedition roster? She was a free spirit, but he didn't get the feeling she slept with just anyone. He watched as she rode back to camp, appreciating the sight of her bosoms bouncing in tempo with the horse's gait. When she disappeared from sight, he stepped up into the saddle and set out to explore the countryside a mite. The more he became comfortable with the land, the better he could scout for Hayden later.

In the span of a half hour, he had become very interested in this job.

By the time he got back to camp, the noon meal was finished and the expedition drivers were getting their teams ready for the next leg of the trip.

"You see any trouble ahead, Mr. Slocum?" Hayden asked.

"Nothing but easy riding," Slocum said. He couldn't help looking toward the photographer's rolling darkroom, where Marlene settled down to continue the trip. A different kind of "easy ride" came to mind. He hoped Hayden didn't notice his glance.

"Excellent, sir, but in a few days that will change. We will reach the southernmost part of Yellowstone, where the mapping is to begin. From that point on, we need to find a way through the challenging landscape."

"Heard tell of geysers and boiling mud holes," Slocum said. "You want to see them or avoid them?"

"An astute question, sir. I would avoid them. However, our artists would prefer to linger and capture their majesty."

"Majesty? A pool of hot mud? Never heard anyone call 'em majestic before."

Hayden laughed.

"Our artists have eclectic tastes." He started to snap the reins on his stallion but Slocum stopped him with one last question.

"You have more artists than Jackson with the expedition?"

"Of course. Gustav Leroq is our primary artist. Mr. Jackson is to concentrate on photography when we reach Yellowstone."

Before Slocum could ask after Leroq, the expedition leader trotted off, yelling at a driver with a balking team that held up the rest of the column.

Slocum caught up with Marlene and was rewarded with one of her sunshine-bright smiles.

"Tonight, John?"

"I'm going to be falling asleep in the saddle if you keep me up too long."

"You certainly were not asleep when you mounted up before. And I somehow doubt it would be possible for me to keep you up *too* long. At least in my opinion."

"Hayden said there was another artist with the expedition."

"There is," she said, frowning. Her sly sex talk hadn't caused the response she had expected.

"Does Jackson own a fancy velvet purple jacket?"

"Mr. Jackson? He prefers earth tones in his clothing. That way the burns and chemical stains from the darkroom don't show. He is usually dressed as you found him while working."

"Where's Leroq?"

"Why, I don't know. I find him an irritating man, so self-absorbed. His claims of artistry certainly do not match his expertise, but you'd think he was the finest painter since El Greco."

"Jackson said he used special cases to carry his paintings."

"Why, of course. He is quite insistent on using the ones made for him in Washington, D.C."

"So Leroq has his own?"

Marlene laughed harshly and said, "He considers everything his own, but I do believe he had some made similar to those William uses."

"I need to scout ahead," Slocum said. He heard her call after him about them getting together later. Under other circumstances, he would have been more excited, but now he thought only of Gustav Leroq—and the Innicks' stolen ruby. He must have been right when he thought only Leroq was involved. If Jackson brought his cases from Washington, he had no need of having more made by the Otter Creek carpenter.

Slocum returned to the camp after sundown. Many of the expedition had finished their chores, eaten dinner, and were unrolling their blankets for some well-deserved sleep. Slocum rode toward the darkroom wagon and saw the rear door open. Marlene and Jackson worked inside, illuminated by the pale light from a kerosene lantern. From what he could tell, they were mixing chemicals likely used to develop the pictures. Whether they intended to work into the night developing photographs Jackson had taken during the day or if this was simply preparation for later wasn't anything he could tell. Riding over and asking was the best way of finding out.

He felt stirrings in the crotch when he saw how Marlene pushed back brunette hair from her eyes, then bent over to lift a case of empty glass bottles. Their first real meeting in the meadow wasn't anything he could easily forget nor was her promise for more such frolicking this evening.

But she would be occupied for some time. That gave him the opportunity to poke around camp. He dismounted and led his horse to a rope corral. After seeing his horse fed, he hobbled the mare and went to find Leroq.

Wandering between the wagons finally brought him to the wagon he had seen earlier with the specially made cases in the rear. He intended to search the crates and then go through the packed goods on either side when he heard a booming voice launch into a bawdy song.

He left the wagon and went to a nearby fire where a dozen men had gathered. On the far side of the firepit, a man in a gaudy purple coat hoisted a bottle and took a long pull before passing it along. He was already so drunk he could hardly sit on the log. He threw up his arms to keep his balance and lost the battle. Tumbling flat onto his back, he lay there laughing heartily. The men on either side grabbed him and pulled him back to a sitting position.

"I do declare, Leroq, that coat of yours shore do feel good," one of the men said. "It's like drapes I saw once in a whorehouse."

"I would never rob a house of ill repute of its curtains," Leroq said, slurring his words. "Rather, they undoubtedly stole one of my jackets after I had exhausted myself pleasuring all their amply endowed ladies!"

This produced a new round of laughter. Leroq launched into a series of increasingly improbable tall tales about his sexual conquests. Slocum didn't believe a one of them. He pushed his way into the circle and watched the artist closely, wondering whether if Leroq got drunk enough, he would flash the huge ruby to brag on his thieving skills. When it didn't happen, Slocum spoke up.

"We can't believe you," Slocum said loudly. "A lover with your skill must have been given something more by his ladies. Something other than a coat made from whorehouse curtains." Slocum intended to provoke Leroq into flashing the ruby, giving some far-fetched story of how he had come by it.

To his disappointment, Leroq went in the other direction.

"Ladies gift me only with their most private of parts. It is I, *Gustav Leroq*, who is lavish with not only my physical endowments but also my presents."

"More than two bits, you mean?" Slocum cut in, intent on goading a confession from the artist. "Or do you give them some piss-poor trinket?"

Leroq took another long drink from the bottle. He wobbled so much both men on either side were hard put to keep him upright. Leroq looked at the finger's worth of amber liquor remaining, belched, then downed it all in a single gulp.

"I am generous beyond my means. I am only a poor artist who—" Leroq's words cut off suddenly as he sagged forward. His two supports let him topple forward. One arm flopped out and landed in the fire.

When no one went to help put out the fiery purple velvet sleeve, Slocum hopped over the fire and dragged Leroq back. He beat out the fire, snuffed a few stubborn embers, then heaved the artist to his feet. With an arm around Leroq's shoulders, Slocum half dragged him away.

"Time for him to sleep it off," Slocum said.

"Damned son of a bitch drunk all the whiskey. We're only a couple days out, and he polished off the whole bottle," complained a man at Slocum's right.

This sparked new discussion, giving Slocum the chance to get Leroq away from the gathering. He shook the man into a half-alert state.

"Where's the ruby you stole?"

"I? I would never steal a ruby. Knew a woman named Ruby. Knew one named Pearl, too. Ruby was prettier."

"You had a sneak thief steal from the owner of a sawmill. What'd you do with the ruby?"

Leroq had passed out. Slocum got him to the wagon and spun fast, releasing the man to flop onto the ground beneath the wagon bed. He dropped to his knees beside Leroq and quickly searched him for the ruby. A gemstone that size would have made a big lump in the man's pocket. Slocum didn't find it, nor had he expected to. After his ribbing around the campfire and excessive drinking, Leroq would have flashed the ruby to bolster his reputation. A man who bragged like he did would have reacted instinctively.

But he hadn't. Slocum had watched carefully, and Leroq never even gestured toward a pocket where the ruby might be hidden.

He left the man snoring on the ground, his pockets turned inside out. Slocum crawled back into the wagon, pushing aside the fancy painting cases to reach the bundles of clothing and other belongings stored toward the front. Slocum undid the first bundle and only found painting supplies. He dropped the tubes of paint and brushes to the wagon bed and worried open a box that held Leroq's gaudy clothing. Bit by bit he went through it, carefully examining every pocket and hunting for seams where the ruby might have been sewn.

As he pried open another box, he heard a muffled gasp. Slocum looked over his shoulder. Marlene Wilkes stood at the rear of the wagon, her hand pressed into her mouth.

She took a step away and shook her head in disbelief.

"You're nothing but a sneak thief! You're robbing a man who's passed out!"

"Marlene, he stole—" Slocum spoke to empty air. The woman had fled into the night. Slocum waited for a hue and cry to go up. When none came, he returned to searching Leroq's belongings.

The last box contained a mortar and pestle like the ones used in pharmacies. He ran his finger in the bowl. It came away gritty. But nowhere did he find the ruby.

Slocum sat on the back of the wagon, his long legs dangling down. He stared at Leroq peacefully snoring as he slept off his drunkenness. Slocum hadn't found the ruby and hadn't gotten anything useful from the artist.

And worst of all, more than the failure to recover the stolen gemstone, Marlene thought he was a sneak thief.

7

Slocum fell asleep worrying about what Marlene might say to Jackson or even Dr. Hayden. Leroq was so soused he had no idea what had happened. For two cents Slocum would have tortured the information from him to find the ruby and get the hell away, but instead, he tossed and turned in his bedroll, and an hour before dawn he came fully awake, six-gun in hand, when a dark shape moved toward where he camped.

"Relax, sir. I wanted to ask you to scout the river ahead and find us a decent ford. My pitiful maps end a mile or two farther."

Slocum put down the six-shooter, rubbed his eyes, and then realized Hayden wasn't firing him but giving him orders for the day's scouting.

"I can get on the trail right away," he said.

"There's no need to be in such a hurry. It takes these sleepyheads an hour after sunrise to get moving."

Slocum had his own reasons for wanting to leave before anyone stirred—before Marlene arose. He enjoyed scouting, and Hayden struck him as a decent sort, intent on his

job and focused on nothing else. But that mapping job would
be threatened by a sneak thief in camp. All Marlene had to
do was tell the expedition leader she had seen Slocum rum-
maging through Leroq's belongings.

Slocum might have sought her out and lied, but that was
wrong. Telling the truth would get him nowhere either. He
didn't want to seem like a bounty hunter out for reward and
nothing more. He frowned as he realized being in her good
graces went far beyond having sex with her again. He liked
her and the way she conducted herself. Being thought of
poorly was a knife wound in the gut.

Was it better that she believed he was a thief or a bounty
hunter? Not once did he consider the easy lie that he simply
sought something in the artist's belongings to help Leroq
with his hangover. Even pushing the lie a bit farther and saying he wanted to get the artist more whiskey wasn't right.

He wouldn't lie. And telling the truth was likely to brand
him as surely in her eyes as someone to avoid. He had joined
the expedition under false pretenses.

"Don't mind," Slocum said, knocking the bugs out of his
boots before pulling them on. "The sooner I get you across
the river, the sooner you can start mapping."

"Oh, I've already begun that shore. Several of my cartographers have improved on maps of this terrain."

"You want me to sketch my route?"

"No need. We are better able to do that chore. Your job
is to find us the quickest way into the heart of the Yellowstone country."

"I'll see what I can find," Slocum promised. Hayden went
off, whistling tunelessly as he prepared for another day of
exploration.

Again Slocum felt the pang of not having found this job
before he promised Innick to return the stolen ruby. He
belonged out in the wilderness, and being at the head of such
an expedition promised to give him everything he had been
missing as a sawmill worker.

He gathered his gear and saddled up. Not for the first time he considered stopping by the darkroom wagon to speak with Marlene, but words wouldn't be enough. She had seen what she'd seen—and he couldn't deny that he would have taken the ruby if he had found it. Convincing her that he would also have dragged Leroq back to Marshal Smith's jailhouse would take more time than he had.

He had been given a mission. Range ahead and find a ford for the expedition.

Slocum chewed on a strip of buffalo jerky and washed it down with occasional gulps of water from his canteen as he rode from camp. The fires had burned low. A few embers cast orangish light that faded to nothing as the sun poked above the mountains to the east. A final look in the direction of Jackson's wagon and Slocum was gone from camp.

"Most excellent work, sir. We can float the wagons across easily. My men are already taking depth readings to put on our map." Dr. Hayden nodded in appreciation of Slocum's quick work in finding the proper crossing of the raging river. Spring runoff proved a larger problem than Slocum had expected, swelling the river and turning the current into a millrace. Anything caught unawares in that current would be swept away or smashed to splinters on rocks just under the surface.

"There's some land ahead I looked over when I crossed earlier," Slocum said. "The road's gone, and it might be better to follow the river downstream a ways."

"We have to push forward here. See yonder pass? If we don't cross there, we have to go north almost sixty miles before we can cross to the eastern side of the mountains."

Slocum had ridden a mile or more past the river and had found what Hayden had not mentioned.

"The geysers and sinkholes I've heard tell of aren't only on the far side of the mountains," Slocum said. "There's a mud field just out of sight you might want to avoid."

"You're saying that it might avail us naught to cross

here?" Hayden rubbed his chin whiskers, then said, "I'll consult with a few of my cartographers. We'll take a look at the mud flats. Preston and Abel have some experience along the Mississippi with sucking mud and driving wagons through such terrain."

Hayden went to recruit the two mapmakers, leaving Slocum to alternately look across the raging river and then back to where William Jackson had parked his darkroom wagon. The rear door stood ajar and sounds of glassware clanking told Slocum that Marlene was inside hard at work securing anything that might spill. He took a few hesitant steps in that direction, intent on telling her why he had joined the expedition and devil take the hindmost when she came out.

For a long heartbeat, they stared at each other. His green eyes locked with her brown. The spark he had felt when they had first met flared—then he realized it was all one-sided. Marlene scowled and pointedly turned her back to him to speak with her employer.

Slocum started to go to her and have it out, but Hayden and two men dressed in rugged clothing trotted up. The cartographers weren't desk-bound bureaucrats. They had the look of men who might have fought to keep wagons rolling along the banks of the Big Muddy.

"I've told them of your concerns, Mr. Slocum. Let's all ride across to investigate."

Slocum had no choice but to go with Hayden and the other two, leaving Marlene to her confabulation with Jackson. There would be time later. When he returned, she might have cooled off a bit.

Then again, she might have decided to tell Hayden what she had seen the night before. Whichever path she took, it lay beyond Slocum's power to change the result. If he made himself useful enough to the expedition, Hayden might overlook the accusation of petty thievery. His best defense lay in finding the ruby and getting Leroq to confess he had taken it back in Otter Creek.

Slocum and the others successfully forded the river and reached the far side.

Preston said, "Can't imagine what that river's like elsewhere upstream. That's one dangerous crossing."

"Not as bad as the one just south of Hannibal," Abel said. The two began a lengthy argument over which crossing was more dangerous as they rode behind Slocum and Hayden.

"They are like that all the time," the expedition leader said with a chuckle. "In spite of such bitter arguments, they are fast friends and their work is superior."

"Seen that in partners, usually prospectors or miners," Slocum said. "It's their way of keeping real arguments at bay."

"I suppose that is so," Hayden said. "Tell me about yourself, sir. How did you come to Utah?"

Slocum carefully spun his history, leaving out details such as being wanted for murdering a carpetbagger judge and his henchman back in Georgia. Hayden took in all he said, not so much to learn about another man's background as to pass the time. He looked around constantly as he rode. Slocum had the feeling Hayden missed no detail of the countryside and would be able to render it all in a map when they stopped to rest.

They reached the edge of the boiling mud flats before Hayden declared a break.

"Well, sir," he said, pushing his hat back up on his forehead as he studied the ground. "You were not exaggerating when you said this part of the trek would be challenging."

Slocum didn't remember using those words. It would be damned hard to drive wagons across the muddy ground where small pits bubbled and boiled constantly.

"Those mud holes are small fumaroles." Seeing Slocum's expression, Hayden explained. "Those are vents for underground steam. Not far below our feet water boils and flows about in unseen rivers. Whenever the surface cracks, the steam rises, then condenses a mite and forms the hot mud pits."

"What do you think of crossing this?" Slocum asked. It was at least two miles to the far side, where rockier ground promised easy driving for the heavy wagons.

"Preston? Abel? Your opinions?"

"There look to be rocky patches where the wagons might roll unhindered," Preston said. He was everything his partner was not. Tall, rangy, he wore his beard full with small beads strung on the longer strands. His quick eyes darted about, and his large hands never stopped moving, whether to sketch out the terrain or simply to flex into balled fists before relaxing.

"Walking the trail will be safer," Abel said. He barely came to his partner's shoulder and looked as immovable as any of the mountain peaks when he stood still. For all his friend's constant movement, Abel could have been a fixture of nature, permanent and capable of withstanding any wind or storm. "See yonder? The sulfur trail?"

"Game trail," Slocum said, having already noticed the tracks left in the yellow, powdery debris. "That leads in the right direction, but what's good for a deer to run might not be large enough for a wagon."

"Abel is right," Hayden said after some reflection. "We leave the horses here and proceed on foot. Be sure to mark our path."

"Preston can mark, I'll be certain the trail is wide enough, Slocum can scout ahead, and you can bring up the rear." Abel tucked away his sketch pad and settled down to wait.

Slocum saw the flow of power between stolid Abel and the more outgoing Hayden. He wondered if Hayden would contradict Abel simply to regain the upper hand. It was his place to give out assignments, not Abel's.

"Let's get to it," Hayden said without any sign of irritation at Abel giving the commands.

Slocum bent and pulled a half-buried stick from the soft earth. He knocked off the dirt and leaned on it to test the strength. The wood had weathered well and provided a decent walking stick. Using it to test the ground where it was especially muddy, Slocum set out, making his way slowly.

For all of Preston's constant movement, he never once urged Slocum to greater speed. Instead, he gathered his rocks and piled them far enough apart to mark a crude road through the mud fields.

Some parts went quickly; others required Slocum to test the ground with his stick, then retreat and find a different, more solid path. After an hour, he came to recognize safe places and those that proved more treacherous. At no time did the others urge him to hurry. He found himself caught up in the trail blazing and enjoying the sense of being part of a team. During the war he had often worked alone as a sniper. The times he had ridden as an officer at the head of a company, the recruits were largely strangers to him and seldom survived more than a week. He had come to regard them as faceless cannon fodder. To get close to any of them, to learn their names, only meant pain when they died in combat.

Riding with Quantrill had been worse. He knew those men because they were so much like him—until their brutality crossed a line where he would not go. So, in the end, even those men had been distant strangers to him.

Working with Hayden and the other two felt easy.

"We're almost to the edge of the mud flats," Slocum called back. "From here to the foothills looks solid. You want to mark the rest of the route or go back to start the wagons rolling?"

Hayden looked up at the sun, pursed his lips in thought, then said, "We'll go back but starting across will have to wait until tomorrow. Getting the wagons on this side of the river might take the remainder of the morning. I don't want to get caught in the middle of these flats at night and have to camp."

"Good idea, Doc," Abel said. He looked to Preston for

approval. Whatever signal passed between them wasn't for Slocum's eyes, but Preston added his assent.

"Let's head back," Hayden said, turning and leading the way across the patch they had spent the day marking.

Slocum brought up the rear now. Preston and Abel walked along the outermost edges of the trail, double-checking their markers. It felt even better being part of a team this thorough. He had scouted for some hunting parties made up of greenhorns who spun good yarns about their prowess. The men on this expedition showed it in their actions and didn't have to brag about their skills.

Their confidence caused Slocum to mentally drift away, back to Leroq and how Marlene had caught him rifling through the artist's possessions. He had no reason to explain himself to her. All he had to do was find the stolen ruby and return it to Innick before his daughter's wedding. But there would be time enough for that.

How did he get back in Marlene's good graces and why was this so important to him? Those questions bedeviled him and prevented him from seeing Abel stray from their marked roadway.

The man slipped in mud and sat heavily amid a loud splash followed by squishy noises. Preston laughed and then shouted a warning to his partner. Abel had flopped over onto hands and knees and didn't see how the ground was turning liquid behind him.

"Geyser!"

Slocum ran forward to pull Abel away from the fumarole now boiling furiously. The sudden eruption of hot water, steam, and mud picked him up and tossed him away as if an artillery shell had exploded.

Stunned, Slocum lay on his back staring up at steam clouds swirling above him. His chest burned where hot water and mud had splashed, and the ground quivered under his back.

The hiss of releasing steam was drowned out by Abel's scream of utter pain.

8

Huge droplets of mud spattered onto Slocum's face, stinging enough to bring him back to full consciousness. He sat up and wiped the mud from his eyes. For a moment he thought he had gone deaf, then realized the roar in his ears came from the geyser sending steam and hot water fifty feet into the air. Pulling down his Stetson to protect his eyes, he worked his way toward the edge of the mud field, where Abel writhed about, moaning.

"Get away from the edge of the hole," Slocum shouted. His voice sounded hollow in his ears, but Abel heard him. The man reached out.

Slocum grabbed the hand. It slipped away. Both were covered in mud. Slocum surged forward and got hold of Abel's coat sleeve. With a powerful yank, he pulled the smaller man from danger.

Only now they were both threatened. The geyser sputtered, then roared to an even more powerful plume. Slocum rolled over Abel to shield him from the worst of the boiling rain hammering down on them.

"Can make it. Got to."

Slocum's back tingled as the hot water and mud tried to work through his coat, vest, and shirt to find naked flesh. He got his feet under him, then pulled Abel to his feet. The man wobbled but kept moving away from the geyser. With his arm supporting Abel, Slocum guided them through the fog of steam and mud until they burst out onto a rocky patch. Only then did he drop Abel and bend over to catch his breath.

"Where's Preston?"

Slocum looked up at a frantic Hayden. The man swiped at the mud on Slocum's face, then moved to repeat the cleaning of Abel's. Abel weakly pushed the helping hand away and looked up at the expedition leader.

"You can't find him?"

"When the geyser blew, he was on the other side—the side with you and Slocum."

Slocum felt the heat from the geyser mounting, but the height of the plume inched back toward the earth. The initial explosion and subsequent steam were fading away. With any luck the geyser would collapse back to the ground in a few minutes. Only Preston might not have a few minutes if he was caught in this torrent.

Pulling his hat down as far as he could and still see, Slocum tugged at his bandanna and fastened it over his nose. The cloth filtered the sulfur-laden air, reminding him he still wasn't back to his usual alert self. He hadn't even noticed the rotten egg smell until he blocked it with the bandanna.

"Slocum, wait, don't!" Hayden's warning fell on deaf ears. Slocum bowed his shoulders, plowed through the dancing curtain of heat, and burst through to the other side.

Preston lay in a pile, half covered with sizzling mud. Slocum protected him from being buried by new mud as he scooped away what had accumulated. The man's coat and shirt had been burned through in places to reveal blistered skin. He had received a worse blast than either Slocum or Abel, although they had been closer to the point of eruption.

"Come on. Can you walk?"

Preston moaned in pain. He tried to stand, but his legs weren't up to the chore. Slocum got the man sitting up, then to his feet. With a quick move, Slocum got the injured man slung over his shoulders. Staggering, he dug his toes into the soft mud and once more burst through the steamy curtain. Both Hayden and Abel caught him as he started to crash facedown on the ground.

"We can get away. Follow the markers," Hayden said.

Slocum felt Preston's weight disappear from his shoulders, but he couldn't move. He sank to the ground, panting. Abel and Hayden carried Preston between them, but Slocum needed help, too. He had reached the end of his endurance.

Hands against the ground, he felt new rumbles, stronger vibrations that had to come before a more powerful eruption. If he stayed, he would be boiled alive, then his body buried in the hot mud. Summoning up strength from deep within his soul, he began crawling. The hissing turned to a roar again as the geyser renewed its assault on sky and earth.

Slocum looked away from the marked roadway and saw ponds rimmed with needles of crystalline sulfur and knew he would die if he tried to take refuge in any of them. The water might protect him from the geyser behind him, but he would be boiled alive if the eruptions spread. He moved faster, distance promising him his only hope of survival. And then he got his feet under him and ran. Hard. So hard he ran past where Abel and Hayden tended Preston.

"Slocum, wait. Don't leave us!"

The anguish in Abel's plea shattered the shell of fear holding Slocum. He slowed and finally turned. Hayden plied his medical skills on Preston while Abel held out his hand in Slocum's direction, urging him to return. Twenty yards behind them the geyser that had caused all their woes sizzled and popped and slowly died. By the time Slocum joined the other three, the geyser had disappeared, leaving behind only a hot fog.

"You saved his life back there. Thanks," Abel said.

"Is he going to make it?"

"I think so. I need to get salve onto his burns. His back is blistered and his hands are charred," said Hayden. He stood and thrust out his hand to Slocum. They shook. "I wondered what sort of man you were, Mr. Slocum, and now I know."

"Is this going to be safe for the wagons?" Slocum asked. His thoughts continued to tumble and twist around. He didn't accept compliments easily, and Hayden's had been sincere. The mission had been to pioneer a trail across the mud flats to the mountain pass.

Hayden laughed at this.

"You are a man directed to his work, sir. I appreciate that. What do you think about using this road, Mr. Abel?"

Abel knelt beside Preston, looking upset at being unable to do more for his partner.

"There's no telling when a geyser will spout off, but there doesn't seem to be any way around. No quick way, and we've got to cover as much territory as fast as we can." Abel looked around, then said, "If we don't stop and keep moving, we can use the marked road."

Shock began to leave Slocum. He felt the tiny burns and the big aches, but his brain still refused to focus properly. All he could think of was Marlene getting trapped in the middle of the boiling mud. And Leroq. If Leroq died out here, the ruby would be lost for all time.

"I agree. Now let's get Preston out of here. And get ourselves out of danger, too."

They took turns carrying Preston, who moaned constantly. As they walked, Slocum eyed every mud hole suspiciously, as if it were waiting for them to be passing nearby before erupting. Although none showed signs of exploding skyward, the bubbles warned of imminent disaster.

By the time they returned to their horses, Slocum had settled down and realized the fumaroles had been churning like this as they had entered. Only his imagination had built possible danger once the solitary geyser had erupted.

"We'll have to tie him to his horse," Hayden said uneasily.

"Belly down is a hard way to ride," Slocum said. From the way Preston drifted in and out of consciousness, he wasn't sure the man could make it back to the wagon train. "We can leave him here and bring the wagons to him."

"An excellent idea, Mr. Slocum. I am the medical doctor. You two return and get the expedition safely across the river, and on the way here. I'll do what I can for him." Abel looked skeptical, but Hayden had only cheering words for him.

"I want to stay, too."

"I'm the newcomer to the expedition," Slocum pointed out, "and the others might not take kindly to me giving orders, even if I explained what happened."

"Go with him, Mr. Abel, and lend support to my order. I suppose I could write it, but that hardly solves the dilemma since so few in the expedition would recognize my handwriting."

"Draw them a map," Abel said. "They all recognize your style."

"True," Hayden said. Then he came to his decision. "Go with Slocum. Get them here as quickly as you can."

Slocum saw Abel getting ready to argue.

"I can fetch them. The drawn map is a good idea," he said.

"I have my sketches here." Hayden pulled a sheaf of pages from his courier's pouch and leafed through until he found one. "This is distinctive. I'll also write a quick note. If necessary, show it to Fenwicke. He's second in command while I am gone from the expedition." He scribbled and handed it to Slocum. "That will have to do, I fear."

Slocum tucked it into his coat pocket and left. He had a long road to travel and probably skeptical cartographers to convince.

"Only one more wagon," a driver said, looking back across the surging river. "Don't know if they can make it without help."

Slocum personally had shepherded four wagons across the ford already. The only one remaining belonged to William Jackson. The photographer worked futilely to attach a floatation device just above the wheels. The darkroom wagon's high profile made it more likely to tip over in the river than the other wagons.

He convinced his mare to cross the river once more. Both he and the horse were drenched from the trips, but Slocum didn't mind. It got the mud off his clothing and the icy water fed by high mountain runoff had chilled the burned spots on his back and hands. He didn't have any special salve, but he felt ready to whip his weight in wildcats again.

Slocum saw how apt that was when Marlene glared at him.

"We don't need your help," she said in a tone that brooked no argument.

Instead of speaking to her, Slocum asked Jackson, "Do you need another pair of hands to get that sack fastened? I haven't seen anything like that in quite a while."

"The prairie schooners were similarly tall and used these to cross the Missouri, or so I am told," Jackson said. "Your help would be appreciated." He glared at his assistant. Marlene turned her nose upward and looked away, arms crossed and the set of her body telling how pissed she was at Slocum.

"I lost count of the wagons," Slocum said. "You the last one?" He stepped back and studied his handiwork. The rawhide strips were secure and the bags—they looked like the bladders of some large animal—flopped about. Once in the river they would rise up, support the wagon, and let Jackson drive it across without overturning.

"Twenty-two ahead of us."

"Who hasn't crossed?"

"You ought to know, Mr. Slocum," Marlene said coldly. "Gustav Leroq left the party while you and the others went off."

"Where'd he go?"

"To paint," she said. He saw the woman wasn't likely to give any more information.

"He does oils. There was a vista a mile or two back that would appeal to Gustav," Jackson said. "I considered a photograph there, but I chose to save my precious plates for later, when we're deeper into Yellowstone."

"You just might sink deep into Yellowstone," Slocum said, noting how the heavy wagon made depressions in the ground twice as deep as the others. It was not only tall and ungainly but heavily laden.

"How far ahead will we camp? I need to be certain all my chemicals are properly stored after our crossing." Jackson looked at the river with some irritation, as if it had been placed there as a barrier to him alone.

"There's a geyser field where Hayden and the others are waiting. You'll camp there, then cross the field at first light."

"Very well. Are you going to come with us?"

"Leroq is alone. He might not be a skilled enough driver to cross the river on his own." Slocum saw how the wagons had cut up the grass and left deep ruts. The artist wouldn't have any trouble finding the trail. Following it might be more of a chore, especially if he didn't reach the rest of the expedition before they crossed the boiling mud flats the next morning.

"Yes, by all means, go find him. He might have something worth stealing, though I am sure you only consider that in the dead of night."

Jackson looked sharply at Marlene, then at Slocum. He started to ask, then shook his head, climbed into the driver's seat, and began the crossing. Slocum watched to be sure nothing untoward happened. In less than ten minutes he caught sight of Marlene leaning out and looking back across the river at him. The distance robbed him of any chance to see her expression, but he doubted she wished him well and would have been happy to see him drown in the raging river.

He pressed out as much water as he could from his

clothing, tended his horse, and then stepped up into the saddle. Following the wagon ruts back proved easy enough, as was finding where Leroq had left the road. Slocum stood in his stirrups and tried to spot the artist ahead. The gathering twilight hid all but the most obvious features in the terrain.

Slocum urged his horse after the wagon. As he hunted for Leroq, he tried to determine how likely it was to reach the expedition camp at the edge of the geyser field before they crossed that deadly barrier. Preston and Abel had done well with the rock markers. He could get across with no trouble, but without him guiding the artist, Leroq might never rejoin Hayden and the others.

Letting him rot in the middle of the fumaroles would be fitting punishment for the theft, but if he had the ruby with him, it would be lost, too. Slocum considered how easily he could pry the gemstone away from the popinjay. If Leroq gave it up out here well away from the rest of the expedition—and Marlene's disapproving glare—Slocum was inclined simply to ride away.

He felt some obligation to Hayden, but he had promised Sean Innick he would recover the ruby.

Idle thoughts wandered through his head as he drifted a bit, considering the chance of getting the ruby back to its rightful owner and then catching up with the mapping expedition later. He wasn't going to remain employed at the sawmill. That had been a job taken because he couldn't find anything else to put some food in his belly.

Mapping Yellowstone appealed to him. And the pay wouldn't matter if he had another five hundred dollars in gold riding in his pocket.

He jerked alert when he heard a horse neigh ahead. The dusk rapidly turned to darkness. The evening star shone brilliantly in the far west, a herald for the rest of the stars.

Then his hand went to his six-shooter because he didn't hear one horse but many.

Riding ahead slowly, straining to see in the dark, he finally made out Leroq's wagon with its specially built cases. The team had been hobbled and nibbled at grass a few yards away. He didn't see the artist anywhere.

But the sound of horses galloping brought him around, peering eastward. If Leroq had intended to paint a landscape, that was the likeliest direction toward the mountains. Slocum put his heels to his horse's flanks and walked in that direction. From the corner of his eye he caught movement. Then he made out the figures ahead.

Gustav Leroq stood surrounded by Indians, and from the sounds of their voices, they weren't any too pleased with finding the artist on their hunting ground.

9

Slocum was no expert but recognized words in Piegan, the Algonquian tongue spoken by the Blackfoot Indians. He realized he had ridden too close, and the Indians had spotted him. He slipped his hand away from his Colt. This hunting party numbered a dozen braves. Shooting it out would be suicidal.

He cursed his bad luck and then he cursed Leroq for good measure. If it hadn't been for the artist's thievery, he wouldn't be in this pickle.

"What's going on?" Slocum called.

"I came out to begin my work. This was an absolutely lovely spot to do a landscape, then these . . . savages rode up screaming and waving their sticks about."

"You're lucky they didn't fill you with arrows." Slocum saw that the hunting party was evenly armed with bow and arrow and old Spencer rifles, likely taken off the bodies of dead cavalry troopers.

He hadn't heard of any trouble with the tribes recently, but he had been toiling away in a sawmill where such gossip meant less than talk of going into town to get drunk and look for whores.

Slocum called out a greeting to the Blackfoot who seemed to be the chief of the party. His instincts were good. The others deferred right away to the tall, muscular man who thrust his rifle high above his head and spoke so fast Slocum had no chance to follow.

"What's he saying?"

"You're trespassing." Slocum's mind raced to find a way to weasel out of getting scalped over such a minor thing. The Blackfoot were territorial and possessive of their hunting grounds.

"I have no intention of killing any small, furry animal for food," Leroq said with some distaste. "I am an artist. I paint! All I need to survive is inspiration, not some morsel of rabbit or haunch of venison."

Slocum knew he had only a small chance if he turned tail and ran, but he couldn't leave Leroq to the mercy of the Indians. Even if the artist tossed him the ruby he'd stolen and proclaimed his guilt, Slocum couldn't abandon him to the Indians. He dismounted and walked to stand a couple feet from the chief. The man was an inch taller than Slocum's six feet and stronger from the look of his thick chest half hidden by a fringed deerskin vest. Any hope of challenging the chief to single combat vanished from Slocum's mind.

Speaking slowly, worrying that he would be misunderstood, he explained that Leroq was a fool, a village idiot among the white eyes, and had come out to smear paint on a piece of paper.

"A wise chief understands when a village must deal with a fool," Slocum said.

"What're you saying?" Leroq demanded. "He's looking at me like I am a madman!"

"Dance around a little. Flap your arms like you're a bird." Slocum saw Leroq's expression of disbelief. "Go on, do it."

Leroq stared in amazement at the circle of Blackfoot, all edging away from him, then began a crazy dance, mocking the Indians. Slocum doubted the Blackfoot caught the contempt Leroq had for them. It all added to the impression of him being the village fool.

"He is crazy," the chief said. "You will take him away?"

"I will," Slocum said. To Leroq he said, "Pack your equipment. They're letting us go. Don't take too long or the chief might change his mind."

"Can I stop this silly dancing?"

"Keep it up," Slocum said, enjoying the artist's discomfort. He watched the artist toss brushes into a box and close it up. The painting he had worked on was almost complete. He took it from the easel, but the Blackfoot chief cried out and grabbed for the painting.

"That's mine!" Leroq started to fight the Indian over the painting, but Slocum clamped his fingers around Leroq's wrist and squeezed hard enough to make him yelp.

"Let him take it. Either that or he'll take your scalp."

Slocum doubted the Blackfoot were interested enough to scalp them. If anything, taking Leroq's scalp would be a disgrace since they thought he was a lunatic.

"Take this as my gift," Slocum said in the Blackfoot dialect, careful not to insult the chief. "He has captured the mountains in his drawing."

He stumbled over the word "drawing" but tapped the edge of the frame to give the Blackfoot chief the idea. The man held up the painting and peered at it in the dark. Slocum knew that they would be dead men if Leroq had tried to paint the images of the Indians themselves, but artistry among the Indians included animals and landscape. From what he could tell, Leroq had rendered the country well.

The Blackfoot chief let out a whoop, held the painting over his head, and spoke too rapidly for Slocum to follow. The braves mounted and soon galloped away in the dark. The chief stared at Slocum, saying nothing, then he mounted and held the painting as if it might come alive at any instant. With another whoop, he wheeled his pony around and followed the others into the night.

"That was my finest work," Leroq said.

"Be inspired that you're still alive. You can do another picture," Slocum said. "Let's get the hell out of here. We've got a lot of travel between now and rejoining the expedition."

"I do not know you, eh, but I do somehow," Leroq said, staring at Slocum in the darkness. "You are the new guide hired to show us only the most scenic areas of Yellowstone."

"I was hired to scout," Slocum said. He considered finding out where the ruby was and putting an end to the charade right now. But the feeling that the hunting party waited just beyond sight wore at him. Better to deal with Leroq and the stolen ruby when they were safe.

"There is something of last night that I do not remember."

"You were drunk. I dragged you to your wagon," Slocum said.

"Ah, a noble companion in wine."

Slocum vaulted into the saddle and pointed to the grazing horses. Leroq bounced from ebullient to surly in a flash. Waiting for the artist to hitch up the team wore on Slocum's nerves but eventually Leroq grabbed the reins and got the horses pulling. His wagon creaked and groaned, then Leroq rattled off without paying any more attention to Slocum.

Following the wagon, Slocum watched their back trail. He had convinced the Blackfoot chief that Leroq was deranged. The Indians would stay away, but all it took was one hothead to think about their hunting ground being violated. A couple scalps dangling from his belt would go a ways toward elevating his prestige and giving him more sway in council.

Slocum urged Leroq to greater speed all the way back to the river.

Slocum let Leroq drive ahead while he guarded their back trail against the Blackfoot. The artist reached the river and was starting across on his own when Slocum caught up.

"You need help?" Slocum called. All he got back was a muffled reply.

He started into the river after Leroq, guiding his horse carefully at the ford. Leroq had followed the wagon ruts left by the expedition, but Slocum saw the man had struck out at an angle rather than going directly across.

"You're too far downriver," Slocum shouted. "Veer back to your right. You're going to be swept away if you get into deeper water."

He cursed as the wagon listed and sideslipped as the dark water pushed Leroq away from the shallows. Slocum kicked at his horse's flanks and entered the cold, rushing stream. Night turned the water to frothy ink. Slocum plowed ahead as the wagon continued to slip into deeper water.

"Leroq, you idiot! Get the team pulling to the right!" Slocum came even with the driver's box and saw Leroq slumped over. The reins were wrapped around his wrists and jerked hard at the artist, threatening to yank him into the water.

If Leroq was thrown into the raging river, he was a dead man.

Slocum jumped, grabbed the side of the wagon, and let his horse flounder ahead to the far bank without him. The horse had made the crossing enough times not to get spooked. But Slocum found himself pinned against the side of the wagon by the powerful current. Every surge in the river slammed him hard enough to jar his teeth. Clawing fiercely, Slocum pulled himself up and over the side into the driver's box in time to grab Leroq. The river finally washed up far enough to catch at the man's gaudy jacket.

The velvet turned leaden as it soaked in gallons of water. If Slocum hadn't grabbed him when he had, Leroq would have been swept away.

"Get down there, you son of a bitch." Slocum threw Leroq to the floor of the driver's box. Water flowed over the unconscious man, promising to drown him unless Slocum did something fast.

Untangling the reins from Leroq's wrists, Slocum began pulling hard to aim the horses to shallower water. The current threatened to spin the wagon around, but Slocum was expert and his firm hand on the reins settled the two horses. They strained so hard one line broke. Slocum had to compensate. Snapping the reins constantly convinced the horses they should keep fighting the current. And then they reached rocky shallows and burst out onto the muddy shoreline.

"Whoa!" Slocum had to brace his feet against the front of the box and use his entire body to pull back before the team stopped. Letting them run wild after escaping the deathly grip of the river could be as dangerous in the dark.

Slocum wrapped the reins around the brake and sat for a moment, shaking in reaction. His arms and shoulders quaked and his legs turned suddenly weak. He leaned forward, grabbed Leroq by the collar of his purple velvet jacket, and heaved the man upright.

Water bubbled from his nose and mouth, then he choked. Slocum dropped him to avoid the torrent if he puked out his guts. Leroq shook and finally collapsed to the floor.

"Get up," Slocum said. When the artist didn't respond, Slocum dragged him up to the seat beside him.

An ugly gash on the side of the man's head showed what the problem had been out on the river. A surge had unbalanced him, and he had struck his temple against the side of the wagon. Knocked out, he hadn't been able to guide the team. If Slocum hadn't been close behind, both wagon and driver would have been lost with no one the wiser as to their fate.

"Wake up. Come on." Slocum shook Leroq but got no response.

He had seen men with head injuries during the war. Worse, he had seen men kicked in the head by a horse. Most of them had never been right again. Despair faded as anger drove him. Leroq had the ruby, and Slocum had promised to return it.

Five hundred dollars. He wasn't going to miss out on such a huge reward. In gold. Not because of a dandy artist banging his head.

Slocum climbed down, caught his horse, and then hobbled the mare with the two from the team so they could graze on grass or go to the river for water if they chose. Then he built a fire, pulled Leroq from the wagon, and laid him out beside it. The man hadn't died, but he wasn't aware of the world around him either.

The fire would dry him out and keep him from catching a chill. Knowing that Leroq wasn't likely to revive anytime soon, Slocum set to searching the wagon for the ruby. An hour later he had poked into every nook and cranny, stopping just short of pulling out the nails and dismantling the entire wagon.

The ruby was nowhere to be found.

Slocum searched Leroq, who moaned and feebly tried to stop him. But the artist never opened his eyes. And still Slocum didn't find the ruby.

The head wound had swollen up to the size of a goose egg. Slocum probed it with his fingers, not caring if he was gentle enough. Leroq winced and tried to shy away but never came to. That told Slocum the man had to sleep off the injury. Jostling him in the back of his wagon to rejoin the expedition wasn't a good idea—Leroq might give up the ghost along the way.

Slocum fixed himself a decent meal using Leroq's larder. He had to admit the man's coffee was better than just about any he had drunk in a coon's age. Then he realized the man could afford the finest since he was a jewel thief.

As he lounged back, Slocum turned that over in his head. Leroq might have kept the ruby, but the rest of Mrs. Innick's jewelry had gone to the thief actually breaking into the house. Gold chains and other semiprecious gems, including a strand of pearls, had to be worth as much as the single ruby, yet Leroq had apparently cared nothing for those. All he had wanted was the ruby.

It made no sense. Slocum finished the coffee, had another helping of biscuits and bacon, sopping up the last of the grease from the frying pan, then lay back. His entire body ached, and he wanted nothing more than to simply be astride his horse and riding to a destination he had chosen. Or riding with no particular destination at all. But the promise he had made chained him as surely as steel shackles.

Slocum awoke as the first light filtered through the trees to caress his face. He sneezed, sat up, and looked around. Nothing had changed from the night before. Leroq still moaned occasionally but had not regained his senses.

Nursing the artist wasn't something that appealed to him. He examined the man's head wound again and decided the swelling had shrunk. He put a cloth soaked in the cold river water on the bump. A tiny smile came to Leroq's lips. This decided Slocum. He worked to make a bed in the rear of the man's wagon, wrestled him onto the pallet, and then hitched up Leroq's horses. With his own horse trailing behind, Slocum began the drive toward the distant mud fields. Turning Leroq over to the expert attention of Dr. Hayden appealed to him more as he drove.

The way was bumpy, in spite of Slocum trying to avoid most of the rocks on the trail he had blazed. When his nostrils flared with the stench of sulfur, he knew the mud flats weren't far away. He found the way increasingly difficult because the earlier passage of the expedition wagons had cut up the soft ground. Water leaked constantly, turning the entire area into rim-deep mud.

In places, Slocum had to fight to keep the team pulling to prevent becoming boggled down. But his skill prevailed and the wagon finally rolled into the rocky area adjoining the broad expanse of seething mud holes where Hayden had camped for the night—the prior night.

Slocum had made good time, but it would be dark in a couple hours. To drive into the mud flats would be folly. If he missed just one marker laid by Preston and Abel, he would wander into unexplored regions. As if emphasizing the recklessness of advancing when darkness would rob him of the trail, a geyser only yards in front of him spewed steam and mud twenty feet in the air.

He went to the rear of the wagon and dropped the gate. Leroq moaned and thrashed about. That was a good sign. The more he moved, the likelier he was to come out of his coma. Slocum reached over and pinched the man's earlobe. If anything brought the artist around, that would do it.

Leroq's eyelids fluttered but did not open. Slocum turned and looked around where Hayden and the others had camped. He wondered where Jackson had parked his darkroom wagon. What had Marlene done? Did she fix food or had she spent her hours inside the rolling photo studio mixing chemicals for later use?

Slocum considered searching the wagon and Leroq again for the ruby, then knew he had found nothing to show the artist ever had the stolen gem. He had even kneaded the paint tubes thinking Leroq might have hidden it there. Most of the paint tubes were already half used. A few glass jars filled with grainy dust of different colors hid nothing inside. Whatever Leroq had done with the ruby, it wasn't here.

The nagging idea that Leroq wasn't responsible kept haunting him. Had the thief seen Leroq and latched on to someone with such an outrageous description to convince Slocum that he was innocent of the theft? That didn't make much sense. Why had the thief held on to the gold and other items but hidden the ruby? Or had he pried it loose and somehow lost it? Better to confess that so Slocum would go off on a wild-goose chase.

Listening to how people spoke had given Slocum the edge more than once in a poker game. The thief's confession had the ring of truth to it. So did his claim that Leroq had taken the ruby.

Slocum built a cook fire and fixed more food from Leroq's stores. He was going to get fat and sassy, at least until Leroq came to his senses. Slocum poured some water into the man's mouth. Getting him to chew didn't happen, so Slocum boiled some oatmeal and fed that to the artist.

After eating, he wandered along the edge of the geyser field, then finally turned in. He unrolled his blanket beneath the wagon and fell asleep with the scent of sulfur in his nose and mouth.

Somewhere after midnight, he thought the entire Union Army had opened fire with an artillery battery. The ground shook and the wagon bounced up off all four wheels. Then came the barrage that forced him to roll onto his belly and curl up to protect himself until the bombardment passed.

Only it didn't die down. It grew in intensity, and Slocum feared for his life.

10

The wagon twisted in ways no wood was meant to bend, and Slocum was tossed up and down repeatedly. He kept curled up in a tight ball as hissing projectiles landed all around. Under the wagon presented some danger if the wagon broke apart, but being out in the open was certain death. He chanced a quick look and saw sizzling shrapnel land in the mud all around. Only the wagon protected him from those missiles.

"Leroq," he muttered. The artist was exposed in the wagon bed. Slocum forced himself to roll out from under the wagon.

Keeping his head down, he scrambled into the bed and grabbed Leroq by the ankles. He pulled hard, sliding the artist along. A piece of burning rock smashed into the spot Leroq had just vacated. It sputtered fitfully like an ember, then went out after charring part of the wood. Slocum had his arms full of the man. He dropped to his knees and heaved Leroq under the wagon. The protection it offered was suspect but better than none at all.

Slocum looked up into the sky and saw that it was filled with fiery shooting stars. He drew back when so many of them crashed into the ground nearby. Daring to grab one, he pulled the hot cinder over to where he could look at it more closely. The particle proved to be a small stone, its exterior melted by extreme heat.

Peering into the night, Slocum traced back the blazing trails left by the eruption to a large fumarole. Burning rock and steam spewed forth to fill the night. When the rock soared high enough, it arched over and came back to earth. What Slocum had thought was deliberate bombardment turned out to be a geyser kicking aloft more than just mud and boiling water.

The rocks stopped falling, leaving only a sizzling rain. All the while Leroq thrashed about.

On impulse Slocum pulled the man close and shouted in his ear, "Where's the ruby?"

He didn't expect much, but to his surprise got a faint reply. Pressing close, he made out the words, "Ashes to ashes, dust to dust . . ."

Leroq hadn't responded to his question but to the hellish world all around them.

Slocum sank back and tried to enjoy the spectacle unfolding before him. However, he had endured too many nights of relentless artillery fire during the war to appreciate this. He fell into a troubled sleep, only to awaken, hand going to his six-shooter. It took him a few seconds to realize the silence had brought him around. Dawn broke and the mud flats stretched serenely.

He crawled from beneath the wagon and examined it. The wood was scarred but intact. The horses had been frightened out of their wits but now sampled a patch of grass that had been over grazed by the other teams when Hayden had camped there. Slocum sucked in a deep breath and choked. Sulfur hung heavy in the air, but only a few pools of bubbling mud betrayed the source.

"Come on," he said, heaving Leroq to his feet and dumping him back into the wagon. "No breakfast. We need to get across this hell plain as fast as we can."

He made what repairs he could on the harness, hitched up the team, and started after the expedition. A few ruts remained from their passage, but the eruption the night before had erased much of the trail. The rock cairns Preston and Abel had so carefully built were scattered back into individual rocks again, making the way difficult.

More than once Slocum stood and studied the land ahead, trying to remember what he had seen before when he had scouted for Hayden. The terrain had shifted with the muddy, blazing geyser eruption, but the mountains ahead gave him a solid landmark. More than once during the day, he had to wait for a geyser to finish spewing steam and mud, but none coughed up the deadly mixture of molten rock and boiling water that had filled the night.

Slocum almost collapsed from strain by the time they rolled onto rockier countryside. But here he located the expedition's trail easily. Hayden had crossed the mud flats, camped, and then pushed on. Slocum read the spoor and knew the others couldn't be more than a day ahead. Hayden had no reason to push hard. He undoubtedly took breaks during the travel to survey and draw his topographical maps. Knowing this kept Slocum moving.

Pushing the exhausted team into the foothills proved worthwhile. As dusk crept up from behind, he crossed the pass to lush plains that stretched as far as the eye could see. Slocum immediately located the expedition not five miles ahead by the smoke from the campfires. His estimate of the distance proved accurate, and he rolled into the camp ninety minutes later.

"Where's Dr. Hayden?" he called to the first man he saw.

"Out with Preston and Abel doing some surveying to the north, along the mountain line," the man answered.

"Leroq conked himself on the head crossing the river and hasn't come to in two days. Is there another doctor in the party?"

"Don't reckon there is," came the answer, "but I was a corpsman during the war. Lemme look at the fellow."

Slocum gratefully turned the artist over to someone better able to deal with his injuries. As much as he wanted to be there when Leroq recovered to question him about the stolen ruby, he wanted nothing more than to get a decent meal and to see Marlene.

"Where's the photographer's wagon? I don't see it."

"Him and his assistant lit out same time as Hayden and the others, only they went south. Jackson said something about Indians."

"What did he say?"

"Didn't hear it myself," the man said, "but he was of the opinion we had some aboriginal company. Doc Hayden was already gone. Fenwicke was left in charge, and he said he don't fear no Indians. He said Hayden ordered us to stay put, and that's what we're gonna do."

"Blackfoot?"

"You mean the Injuns? Can't say." The man rummaged through Leroq's food. "He been eatin' this or have you been chowin' down?"

"Me," Slocum admitted. "All he's kept down is water and boiled oatmeal."

"Better 'n nuthin', I reckon."

"Where's Fenwicke to be found?"

"Up ahead, easternmost wagon." The man turned to doing what he could for Leroq, leaving Slocum to ride to the edge of camp in search of Hayden's assistant.

He found the man hunched over a drafting table supported by two large rocks. He didn't even look up as Slocum dismounted. Firelight cast a dancing orange shadow over the map Fenwicke toiled on. Slocum had the feeling the man could work in complete darkness from the way he concentrated, his nose only inches over the map.

"When's Hayden due back?"

Fenwicke looked up. He pushed his pince-nez higher on his nose and blinked hard.

"No way to tell."

"I fetched Leroq back. He's been banged up some. Fellow on the other side of camp's taking care of him."

"Leroq? Oh, the fancy-ass artist. Good, good. Now I need to get back to work." Fenwicke ran his finger down a column of numbers on a sheet of paper tacked to the map and started to translate them into actual contours.

"Heard tell the photographer went south."

"That's my recollection."

"Leroq ran into some Blackfoot. A hunting party on the other side of the mountain. If there's one party out, there might be others. Did Jackson know that?"

"If he did, he didn't confide in me. He's a tad close-mouthed. Goes with being an artist and photographer. Find something worth painting or shooting, you don't tell anyone fearin' they'll get there first. Not like making maps. We share every detail. Have to. The government expects accurate maps. That's what they're payin' for." Fenwicke looked up, adjusted his eyeglasses again, and said, "Are you going to bother me any more? Hayden wants this done by the time he gets back with more readings."

Slocum stewed at how little Fenwicke knew of the others in the party. Hayden didn't have to report to a subordinate, but Jackson ought to have let Fenwicke know more about his side trip. After all, he was taking Marlene into dangerous territory.

If he even realized it was more dangerous because of the roving bands of Blackfoot.

Or he could be inventing trouble that didn't exist. Slocum found a spot where he could pitch camp for the night, fixed a small meal, and fell into an exhausted sleep. The sounds of others moving about in camp awoke him the next morning. He stretched and wondered at how long he had slept. This was unusual for him since he usually awoke before sunup.

"You're lookin' a sight better than last night," Fenwicke said, wandering by. The man was dressed in jodhpurs and boots laced up over his calves. His shirt was festooned with pockets stuffed with pencils and wads of paper. He wore a bubble-like helmet with a broad brim in front and back that Slocum thought might have been British. He wasn't interested enough to inquire.

"Feeling better, too," Slocum said. "Any word from . . . Jackson?" He wanted to ask about Marlene Wilkes but didn't feel right coming out and saying the words. She had a reputation to keep up. With him being such a newcomer to the expedition, he wanted to keep gossip to a minimum.

A knot formed in his belly as he remembered how she had given him such a cold stare the last time he had seen her riding away in the darkroom wagon. Chances were good she didn't need his help—in any way.

"The artists head out for days on end. Sometimes they're gone for a week. Dr. Hayden always lays out our route for them so they can catch up. We might spend a week in one camp while surveying, so they don't have trouble catching up."

"What did he tell them about the expedition's route?"

"Well, Slocum, not a whole lot since you're our scout. It's up to you to range out, find the road, then report back to Doc Hayden with that information so he can tell everyone else."

"That means Jackson will return here since he wasn't given any other route."

"Could mean that. Could be that Hayden thinks Jackson is experienced enough to follow our tracks as we push on. Can't say since he didn't confide any of that to me." Fenwicke started to walk on, stopped, and asked, "You going out to find our route?"

"Hayden didn't tell me where he intended to go."

"He went north. You might take that as a hint. If nothing else, you can track him down and ask him."

That struck Slocum as sensible. After he ate breakfast, he packed his gear and rode south. After William Jackson— and Marlene.

Slocum grew edgier as he rode. The darkroom wagon left distinctive tracks—and the tracks following the wagon were equally distinctive. The unshod ponies paralleled the wheel imprints. Slocum pictured the Indians following at a distance where Jackson or Marlene would never notice. But had they overtaken the photographer?

He rode faster and found the empty wagon just after dark. He didn't see any evidence a campfire had been built or any of the cloth-wrapped food packages tucked away inside the wagon had been opened recently.

Circling the wagon, he found footprints leading away. Getting down on hands and knees to better see the imprints in the dark, Slocum sucked in his breath when he realized these had been left by Marlene. Moccasined feet didn't follow. Those prints circled the woman's. He knew because some of her tracks came down on top of an Indian's, showing she followed him. In other places moccasins stomped down on her tracks. The mixture could only mean Marlene had gone with the Indians.

Slocum doubted they could have gone far if both Marlene and the Indians walked. He checked his Colt Navy, then did as good a job as he could to follow the trail. Slocum lost it within a hundred yards.

Momentarily disheartened, he stood, closed his eyes, and let his other senses do the work for him. A faint sound came to him. Indians speaking. He turned slowly in that direction, then took a deep breath and caught the scent of burning pine. His steps took him that way before he opened his eyes. The darkness wasn't as complete as it had been. A sliver of moon in the sky illuminated the way toward the Indian camp.

He advanced more slowly when he reached a spot where he could hear distinctive voices. The cadence of speech and occasionally identified words told him this was a Blackfoot camp. Since he had crossed the mountains, he doubted it was the same hunting party that had found Leroq. The entire tribe might be moving about, hunting and looking for a spot to make a more permanent summer camp.

The curls of smoke rising against the stars sent him to the ground. He wiggled forward on his belly, alert for sentries. To his surprise, the Blackfoot hadn't posted guards around their camp. He slipped within a dozen yards and had a good view of the camp where tepees had been pitched. The scent of fresh meat cooking made his nostrils flare.

This was a large camp but hunting parties had brought back sufficient food to maintain it. From the layout, this might be the summer site for almost a hundred braves and squaws.

Slocum heard a commotion farther around the perimeter of the camp and made his way to a spot behind a fallen log where he could see a circle of braves. From the headdresses these were the senior chiefs in the tribe. A pipe worked its way around the circle as they discussed some weighty matter. Strain as he might, Slocum couldn't make out enough words or overhear anything at all said by several warriors who sat with their backs to him.

Instead of what should have been a solemn discussion, a few of the braves laughed loudly. They were cracking jokes and enjoying themselves, in spite of being in a council. Then the men fell silent as a young brave came from deeper in the camp.

Slocum caught his breath. The brave held on to Marlene Wilkes's arm, steering her toward the elder chiefs.

As she was pushed to the ground just outside the circle, the Indians began chattering all at once, shouting down one another and gesturing wildly. Slocum had no idea what was going on, but it had to do with Marlene.

He had to admire her calm. She looked composed and let the tumult flow around her. Turning to the brave who had escorted her to the circle, Marlene spoke in a low voice for some time. The brave then waited for the chiefs to fall silent, then spoke clearly enough for Slocum to catch enough of the words to know he had to act fast.

The word "capture" was repeated many times, as was "imprisoned" and a phrase that Slocum took to mean that the Great Spirit would never smile on someone again. He had to believe that meant the Blackfoot had taken Marlene as a slave.

He almost betrayed himself when the brave pulled Marlene to her feet and steered her away from the circle, going deeper into the camp. Slocum touched his six-gun and knew that wouldn't be the way to rescue the woman. He had to sneak into the Blackfoot camp and somehow get her away without anyone knowing.

How he could ever do that was beyond him. He stood and, taking advantage of shadows, worked his way toward the tepee where he thought Marlene had been taken. Getting away with his scalp might be hard. Getting away with Marlene looked like it would be impossible, but he had to try.

11

Most of the Blackfoot were gathered around fires, telling their tales of the hunt. Others had disappeared into their tepees. Still, Slocum felt as if every eye was on him as he made his way across stretches of open camp, hunting for the tepee where Marlene had been taken.

But if even one warrior spotted him, the outcry would bring down such destruction on him that he would be lucky to get off even a single shot in reply. Nervous as a long-tailed cat by a rocking chair, he made his way toward a hide dwelling. He drew his thick-bladed knife from the sheath in his boot and cut a small opening in the wall. He had difficulty seeing anything inside. The fire had died down and curls of lazy white smoke blocked his view of the occupants. Moving a quarter of the way around the tepee's circular base, he repeated the cut in the hide.

He caught his breath. Marlene sat to one side with a guard near the entrance. Slocum tried to figure out how he could enter, remove the guard, and get her to freedom. His problem lay in getting into the tepee before the brave saw him. The man sat cross-legged, looking very alert. For her part,

Marlene faced the brave, studying him. Slocum hoped she didn't make the mistake of thinking she could swarm over the Blackfoot and escape that way. But if she tried, it might give him the chance to clobber the brave so Marlene could get away.

Nothing recommended itself to him other than a bit of subterfuge. He moved around until he was near the opening, then coughed out the few words of Blackfoot he knew. When the guard didn't come to investigate the odd sounds, Slocum repeated them, louder.

This time the guard replied with a nonstop stream of words that flowed faster than Slocum could ever hope to understand. He couldn't even get the gist of what the Indian said, so he scratched his hip against the hide wall, pressing in so the brave couldn't miss the bulge from inside.

This produced the result he wanted. The Indian came out, but he had to duck down to get through the doorway. Slocum balled his hands into fists and brought both down on the back of the man's neck with as much force as he could muster. The Indian crashed to the ground. Slocum wasted no time grabbing him by his hide vest and dragging him back into the tepee.

Marlene looked up, eyes wide.

"What are you doing? You hit him!"

"We've got to go!"

"You assaulted him. You—"

Slocum wasted no more time arguing with her. He clamped his hand over her mouth to silence her. She fought, her fists futilely hammering at him. He swung her around.

"Calm down. If they hear, they'll have my scalp. What they'll do to you will be even worse."

Rather than calming so she would go with him, Marlene fought harder. Slocum had no time to argue with her. He clamped forefinger and thumb over her nose and pinched. With his hand over her mouth, he cut off her air. She continued to struggle, but this only caused her to pass out more quickly. He counted this as a blessing.

He dragged her outside, took a quick look around, and then hoisted her over his shoulder as if he carried a sack of potatoes. Retracing his steps, he got beyond the perimeter of the camp but knew it wouldn't be long now before the brave recovered and sent up the cry. The entire camp would be after him and Marlene in a few minutes.

"Come on, you have to walk. I can't carry you. We have to run."

"Run?" the woman mumbled, still groggy. "No. Don't wanna run. Stay. Pictures."

"To hell with pictures. The Blackfoot took you as a hostage. You were going to be a squaw for one of their warriors, if you were lucky. If you weren't, you'd be given to a squaw to use as a slave. Eventually, the entire tribe would have used you." He shook her until her eyelids flicked and her eyes came open. They focused slowly.

"You kidnapped me! Not only are you a thief, you're—I don't know what you are!"

"Is Jackson in the camp, too? Or did they already kill him?"

"What are you talking about? He made a deal with them to take portraits. He's going to photograph an entire encampment. Those photos will be of great interest to anthropologists in years to come."

"The Blackfoot are letting him photograph them? They think that steals their soul, and they won't be able to get into the happy hunting ground when they die."

"You don't know what you're talking about." She crossed her arms and tried to turn away in high dudgeon, but she eased back around to look hard at him. "Did you mean it about the Indians thinking photography steals their souls?"

"I can't believe the Blackfoot are letting him do this. Where is he?"

"Why, they took him to another camp. A Crow encampment and showed him where to set up his equipment. Come sunup he'll capture that camp in all its primitive glory."

"The Blackfoot took him to a *Crow* settlement?" He felt as if someone had punched him in the gut. "The Crow and the Blackfoot are mortal enemies."

"Why would they do that? It doesn't make any sense."

"They don't care if Jackson is killed. He will be, but the more photos he takes, the more Crow souls that will be lost. The Blackfoot wouldn't mind it if all their enemies lost their souls."

"That is a bit far-fetched, don't you think?" She sounded a bit skeptical, but only a little bit. The reality began to dawn on her.

"Which way did they take Jackson?"

"South, about two hours ago. You're not lying, are you?"

Slocum had nothing to gain by lying. He said nothing as he considered what had to be done. His mare couldn't support his and Marlene's combined weight. He might steal an Indian horse. There wasn't any way he could anger them more than taking a prisoner out from under their noses. But outrunning the pursuit wasn't likely to happen.

Worse, where did he go? If he led the Blackfoot back to the expedition, the Indians would kill everyone there. And that did nothing to help William Jackson. The Crow would certainly kill him when they discovered what he was up to. The photographer likely wasn't even armed, or if he was, he carried a pistol only to defend himself against snakes and other small varmints.

"I have to get you back to the tepee. When they discover you're gone, there's no way they won't find you. They are masters at tracking."

"But what about the brave you knocked out?"

"I'll take care of him. First, we've got to get back. Can you walk fast and silent?"

"I . . . yes," she said, her resolve firming.

Slocum set out without saying another word. Time was as much an enemy as the Indians. He had to admit, if he was right, the Blackfoot were shrewd. Get the Crow all riled up over the photographer because he had stolen their souls. This was as good for a Blackfoot warrior to know as if he had run a knife through a Crow's heart.

The circle where the chiefs sat had diminished. Some of them had gone to their tepees. Slocum hoped the chief responsible for Marlene hadn't already gone back. There would be two dead men, if so. He came to the rear of the tepee where she'd been held and pressed his eye against one of the slices he had made in the thick hide wall.

"Is it safe?"

"Come on," he said, grabbing her wrist and pulling her along. Neither of them would be safe unless he worked some kind of miracle. Even if he rescued Jackson, what then? Slocum didn't have a good answer.

He almost shoved her over the still unconscious brave and into the tepee. Marlene stumbled and went to her hands and knees. She quickly turned over and stared at him.

"What do I tell them when they ask where he is?"

"Tell them you think he went out to pizzle and never came back. Tell them he had a bottle of whiskey. Tell them whatever you want but don't be too sure about anything."

He grunted as he got his arms around the brave's chest and heaved the man upright. He felt a light touch on his arm and looked. Marlene's hand shook.

"We're going to be all right, aren't we?"

"Right as rain. Remember. Play dumb. You don't know anything about what happened to this one." With another grunt, Slocum had the Blackfoot over his shoulder.

He remembered how light Marlene had seemed. The brave had to weigh half again as much. Slocum stumbled a few steps, got his balance, and then ran into the night. He heard the woman sob once, then nothing.

She'd be all right. Their lives depended on her ability as

an actress. If she so much as hinted that she knew what happened to the guard, she was dead.

Slocum didn't like what he had to do, but his life—and Marlene's and Jackson's—depended on it. When he had gone a fair distance from the camp, he found a shallow ravine and rolled the Indian into it. He slowly drew his knife. There wasn't any other way. He had done worse, far worse, in his day. A single quick thrust ended the brave's life. Then Slocum worked to cover the body with rocks and dirt kicked in from the low banks of the ravine.

Panting from the exertion, he raced back to his horse and stepped up. Finding and following Jackson's trail in the dark was impossible. He had to rely on luck. After he circled the Blackfoot camp, he got his bearings on the North Star and kept it at his back as he rode into the dark, his only light from the sliver of moon.

Jackson might have had a two-hour start, but it took Slocum until sunrise to find the man and where he had set up his camera. Jackson hummed to himself as he laid out his carrying cases for unexposed photographic plates, keeping them close at hand so he could take a picture, remove the plate, and insert an unexposed one with a minimum of effort.

His camera was directed at a narrow draw. Just beyond Slocum saw the edge of the Crow camp. Already they were stirring, preparing meals, and getting ready for a day's hunt. What they hunted would depend on how successful Slocum was in stopping Jackson. Once the Crow spotted him, his life would be forfeit.

Slocum had to wonder if the Blackfoot were right and that the camera took a man's soul. If so, a considerable number of the Blackfoot's bitter enemy would be bereft and doomed to roam as wandering spirits once their bodies died. Any hope of being reunited in death with their clan would be dashed.

He started to yell to the photographer to get down, then saw he was too late.

"Here, look this way!" Jackson called to a band of three Crow. These weren't hunters. They had war paint smeared on their faces, bodies, and horses.

Slocum didn't bother trying to stop Jackson. Let him rob the Indians of their souls, if the camera had that power. The photographer took the picture. For a moment the three mounted Crow warriors simply stared. Then they exchanged looks of pure horror. One wheeled his pony about and raced back to his camp at the other side of the draw, shrieking in fear.

The remaining two lifted war lances and charged at Jackson. The photographer thought it was all part of the show. The Blackfoot had doubtlessly told him this had been arranged.

Slocum whipped out the Henry rifle from its saddle sheath and began firing. The range was too great for accuracy, but he got lucky. One slug hit the lead Crow's horse and caused it to stumble in front of the other, sending them both down in a heap.

"Marvelous," Jackson said, snapping another photo and working furiously to reload his camera.

Slocum galloped ahead. His aim was a little better now, but firing from horseback at a full charge prevented much in the way of marksmanship. He emptied his rifle's magazine and kept the Crow from mounting a new attack on Jackson. Then Slocum was close enough to draw his Colt and fire.

He fired his first round at less than ten feet from the leading Crow. The slug caught the man just under the chin, snapped his head back, and sent him to the ground, dead before he hit. The other warrior brought his lance around and heaved it. Slocum threw up his left arm to deflect it. He winced as the tip cut into his forearm. But the deadly thrust missed him.

He galloped past the Indian, wheeled about as hard as he could, and fired the rest of his rounds into the brave's back as he rushed for the unarmed Jackson.

The photographer took another picture, then moved from behind the camera to stare down at the dead body at his feet. He looked up at Slocum.

"You shot him. He's dead. The other is, too!"

"Get your horse. We don't have but a minute or two before the whole damned Crow nation is on our necks."

"But they were only posing. This was like a play for me to photograph."

"The Blackfoot lied to you. They wanted you to steal their enemies' souls and didn't care if the Crow killed you or not."

"This is ridiculous, sir. I—"

Slocum fought to reload his Colt while his horse tried to rear. There wasn't time to stuff fifteen rounds into the Henry. A desperate look over his shoulder told him that they had only minutes before the Crow came after them in a wave that could never be successfully repelled.

"Mount up or die right here."

"My plates."

"To hell with them. Do they mean more than your scalp?"

"Yes!" Jackson grabbed the wooden case and awkwardly carried it to his horse. "What about my camera?"

"Either ride or die where you stand," Slocum said. He got off a couple shots intended to slow the attacking Crow. He might as well have spit at them. They were fired with righteous anger, and nothing would slow them short of a mountain howitzer.

Even that powerful piece of artillery might not be enough. The Crow were *mad*.

Slocum bent low and scooped up a rifle dropped by one of the dead Crow braves. He twisted about and fired until it came up empty, which was far too soon. There had been only four rounds in the magazine. He cast the rifle aside and put his head down. Heels raking the flanks of his horse, he rocketed away. To his relief he saw that Jackson had mounted and rode like the wind. Somehow, the man held on to his photographic plate case as his horse built speed to a full gallop.

"We can't keep this up long," Slocum said. "Our horses will die under us if we do."

"It's miles back to the Blackfoot camp."

Slocum knew that. He also knew that Marlene was still being held prisoner. She might have lied her way out of being punished for her guard's departure—but she would be tortured if they happened to find the man in the shallow grave with his throat slashed.

"Down there, into the gully," Slocum said. He slowed and let his horse pick its way down the crumbling embankment.

"Why? We'll be trapped there. No way to run if they get around us."

Slocum knew the Crow might reach the bank and fire down on them. The high dirt walls afforded some protection, though. As he hurried along the graveled gully bottom, he took a deep sniff.

"Sulfur. There must be a mud pit or geyser somewhere near."

"What good will that do us?" Jackson fought to keep from dropping the wooden case.

"Anything that slows the Crow down is good for us." Slocum saw the gully wall on the far side slowly turn into open plains. Not a mile off bubbled one of the mud pits. This one had a steady spewing fountain of steam rising from it.

"If we get to the other side, we'll be hidden," Jackson said. "An excellent idea, sir."

Slocum didn't bother telling Jackson that the Crow wouldn't be put off the trail that easily. But if they had a curtain of steam between them and the pursuing Indians, that made an accurate rifle shot that much more difficult and increased their chances of staying alive to see another sunrise.

He just wasn't sure what those chances really meant in the long run.

His horse had begun to tire when they reached the muddy bank of the fumarole. The mare tried to rear when a new plume of steam hissed skyward. Through the curtain of white fog Slocum saw that the Crow were narrowing the distance between them.

"That way," he said. "Go straight away from the geyser. Keep it at your back."

It would delay the Crow another precious minute or two. That was all Slocum could hope for. Delay. But the eventual resolution crushed in on them like the jaws of a closing vise.

The Crow circled the geyser and thundered down on them, not even bothering to shoot now. They had their war lances out. They might count coup first, then use those wicked spears. Or they might simply get close enough to skewer Slocum and Jackson.

The tactics didn't matter. The result would be the same either way.

Slocum drew his Colt and prepared to sell his life as dearly as possible.

12

"We're going to die," cried Jackson. His horse stumbled from exhaustion. "What can we do?"

"Go down fighting," Slocum said. He tossed Jackson the rifle. "Load that." He rummaged through his saddlebags and found a box of cartridges. He didn't bother to see if Jackson knew how to do this simple chore. The Colt in his hand commanded his full attention.

Slocum dismounted and steadied his six-shooter as the lead Crow warrior whooped and hollered, waving his war lance. With a steady pressure, he pulled back on the trigger. The six-gun bucked with familiar force. And Slocum felt the shot was good. He had developed a sense knowing when he had made a good shot and when he hadn't. This felt like an on-target shot.

He waited to see if the Crow reacted. The shot felt good, but the Indian rode on, as if nothing had happened. When the warrior raced past, slashing with his lance, Slocum saw the tiny red spot on the man's war-painted chest. He had been hit but was so fired up, he didn't even feel it.

As the Indian raced past, Slocum turned and fired again.

This time the Crow knew he had been hit. The bullet struck him in the middle of the back. From the way he flopped off his horse, Slocum had shattered the warrior's spine. But he had no time to appreciate the second shot. Two more braves rushed at him.

He emptied his six-shooter and missed with the remaining shots. He readied himself to grab for a lance and maybe pull the warrior off his horse. The crack of a rifle from behind saved him the need to deal with the nearest warrior. The Crow grabbed his head and fell from horseback. Jackson had not only reloaded but had found the range. He might not be a crack marksman, but his target was close enough that he didn't have to be.

The third Crow hunkered down, a tomahawk swinging in vicious arcs as he rode down on Slocum. Only quick reflexes and a bit of luck saved him from having the sharp-edged weapon take off the top of his head. Then the warrior galloped past. Jackson fired several times, missing with every shot.

Slocum considered taking the rifle from the photographer, then decided reloading his six-shooter was a better move. Let Jackson do what he could with the weapon.

"There must be a dozen more coming after us," Jackson said. He waved the rifle in the direction of the war party.

"Watch the one that got past us. He'll be coming back anytime now." Slocum tried to find where the Crow with the tomahawk had gotten off to, but he was nowhere to be found. He would have worried about that but the approaching war party took his full attention.

He saw his death coming at him as hard and fast as their horses could be ridden.

More rifle reports sounded. Slocum thought something was wrong—or different. He turned to Jackson and found himself puzzled. The photographer struggled with a round that had hung in the breach.

"Who's shooting?"

"Not me," Jackson said. "I can't pry out the punk round."

Reports from rifles mingled with those from six-shooters. Then the source rode into view. A Blackfoot war party had ambushed the Crow. Whether this had been part of the plan from the beginning or was simply a bit of lagniappe didn't matter now. The Blackfoot attacked the Crow and saved Slocum and Jackson from immediate death.

Slocum knew this would be a short-lived victory for the two white men since the Blackfoot had no reason to keep them alive.

"Slocum!" Jackson thrust the rifle in the direction of a mortal fight not twenty feet away. The Blackfoot chief fought with a Crow warrior—and was slowly losing.

The Crow was stronger and younger. He forced his opponent back, then hooked his leg and sent the Blackfoot tumbling helplessly to the ground.

"Let me have that!" Slocum grabbed the rifle from Jackson's numbed fingers.

"The cartridge is still jammed!"

Slocum didn't intend to use the rifle to shoot the Crow. Swinging the rifle over his head, he ran forward. The metal barrel smashed into the Crow's wrist, knocking the knife from his hand. Slocum recovered his balance and swung back. This time the barrel caught the brave just above his right eyebrow. The Crow's head snapped back, and he stumbled a pace.

The Blackfoot chief surged to his feet. With the speed of lightning, he had out his knife—and used it to devastating effect. The Crow grinned from a second mouth, his throat cut ear to ear. The Blackfoot stepped away, stared at Slocum. There wasn't any emotion in his gaze. No gratitude, no fear, no hatred, nothing. With a loud war whoop, he whirled around and ran off to engage other Crow fighters.

Slocum wasn't sure if that was good. He returned to where Jackson stood, mouth agape.

"You hit him."

"Knocked the jammed round out." Slocum tossed the rifle back. The photographer caught it awkwardly, stared into the breach, and then smiled crookedly.

"I didn't know that was how you got a stuck cartridge out." He laughed. He kept laughing until he was close to hysterical.

By the time Jackson had himself under control, the battle had ended with the Crow in full retreat.

"You be sure to tell the chief you stole many Crow souls," Slocum said. "That's about the only way we're going to keep our scalps."

"What of Marlene?"

"She was safe in the Blackfoot camp last I saw."

"You were in the camp with her?"

Slocum silenced the photographer with a cold glare when the Blackfoot chief strutted over, his chest thrust out and a Crow scalp in his hand. He stopped in front of Slocum and stared at him with his unfathomable expression, then held out the scalp for Slocum to take. When Slocum took the scalp and shook it high above his head while he let out a whoop of joy, the Blackfoot's expression changed. He grinned.

"How barbaric," Jackson muttered. Slocum ignored the man.

Against all odds, they had prevailed. He swung the bloody scalp around to be sure all the gathered Blackfoot braves saw the trophy. Then he tucked it under his gun belt.

"My noble companion has also stolen souls from the Crow. He has taken pictures!" Slocum wondered if anyone knew enough to translate for the ones who didn't speak English.

A low murmur passed through the assembled warriors, then a new shout went up.

"You're a hero, too," Slocum told Jackson, speaking out of the corner of his mouth. "Try to look heroic."

Jackson hesitated, then walked about with his thumbs tucked into the armholes of his vest, head back, chin thrusting upward and hips well forward as if he led a Fourth of July parade.

"We need to get back to the Blackfoot camp and get Marlene out," Slocum said.

"If they've harmed her—"

"They wouldn't," Slocum said with more confidence than he felt. So many things could have gone wrong with his scheme. Returning her to captivity had been the only way he had seen that might work. Now that he and Jackson were considered great Crow killers, they might rescue her. If the dead brave had been found, her captivity might have ended abruptly.

Together, riding side by side on their way back to the Blackfoot settlement, Slocum and Jackson spoke in guarded tones.

"It's best if I claim her as my squaw," Slocum said.

"She would never abide by that!"

"Whoever lays claim to her will have to fight for her. If a brave has taken a fancy to her, he might already have her in his tepee."

"They wouldn't. I won't allow it! I'll claim she is mine. That will settle the issue."

"The only way of getting property back is to fight to the death. But don't get all hot under the collar. Not yet. It's possible she hasn't been claimed by any of them. They've been busy making mischief with the Crow."

Slocum wondered if the man he had killed might have taken her as his squaw, only to get his throat slit before claiming his husbandly due. With the Crow raid so soon, even if they had found the body, the Blackfoot might not have cared about a solitary white woman. With even more luck, the Indians might think the dead warrior had been killed by a Crow scout.

As they rode into the encampment, women and children came out. A few older men came out. Those who might otherwise have been out with the war party hobbled or waved stumps about, showing their debilities. Slocum glanced at Jackson, who grinned foolishly. He was basking in the adoration of so many people, even if he thought of them as barbarians.

To these barbarians he was a conquering hero.

"We have to endure a feast," Slocum said. "This might take days."

"Marlene is our first priority."

"We go along with whatever plans they have. There's no way to sneak away from them and not have a couple dozen warriors come after us."

"They are rather savage fellows," Jackson said. "There isn't any likelihood the expedition could fight them off."

"We have to leave with the Blackfoot's good wishes. We need to warn Hayden that the Crow are on the warpath, too."

"We are heading north, away from the other camp. Will that be to our benefit?"

"Likely, it will," Slocum said. Having the Blackfoot between the mapping expedition and the Crow kept the peace in ways he didn't want to think about. The Crow would care less about a white man's wagon train and more about another tribe intent on killing them. Only if the crow needed the livestock from the expedition would they attack.

Slocum and Jackson were buffeted about when they dismounted. Every Indian in camp wanted to touch them, to share in their glory. Slocum took it stolidly, but Jackson seemed to enjoy the attention. When the chief took Jackson aside, Slocum saw the opportunity to slip away and find Marlene. She sat disconsolately in the center of the tent where he had left her. As he pushed through the flap, she looked up. Hope flared, then faded.

"What are they celebrating? They captured you, didn't they? They know what you did to the guard."

"Hush," Slocum said. Few of the Blackfoot spoke English, but he didn't want to risk having one of them overhear.

"I don't know if it would be smart for you to come join the feast."

"I won't do any such thing. You are a terrible man."

Slocum wasn't inclined to argue the point with her. He was a terrible man and had done terrible things, many of them within the past few hours.

"I'm still your only way out of here safely," he said.

"I'd rather die."

"There are things the Blackfoot can do to you that will make you cry for death," Slocum said. "You don't want to find out what they are. Now follow me, stay three paces behind, and keep your head down. Don't say a word unless Jackson or I speak to you."

"William! He's in camp! Take me to him immediately."

"Only if you do as I told you."

"You're a horrid man, John Slocum."

He wasn't going to deny that. Right now, he just wanted to get out of the Indian camp with his scalp.

Not even realizing he'd put that thought into action, he touched the Crow scalp he had tucked into his gun belt. Marlene saw the motion, stared for a second, then realized what it was. She turned pale and almost lost her balance in a faint. Slocum caught her, aware of how natural it seemed for him to have his arm around her waist, her body pulled close. She didn't even struggle as he held her until color returned to her cheeks.

"What else are you capable of doing?" she said in a choked voice. Marlene pointedly looked away from the bloody scalp.

"Whatever it takes to get you away from here." He swung her around, made sure she had good footing, then left the tepee.

To his surprise, she put up no argument about walking behind him. A few squaws and not a few braves watched in silence as they made their way back to the council fire. Slocum had to restrain Marlene to keep her from racing to Jackson's side.

"Sit behind him," Slocum said in a low voice. "Follow his lead."

The woman gladly obeyed and dropped to her knees behind Jackson. The photographer spoke at length to her. Slocum saw the change in her expression as repeatedly she glanced in his direction. The anger and horror faded to something he couldn't define, but she no longer had the combative attitude that might have gotten them all killed.

The victory celebration went on for some time, but when the huge fire began to crumble into glowing embers, the chief stood and walked away. Those around him followed, leaving Slocum, Jackson, and Marlene with a handful of younger braves.

"What now?" asked Jackson.

"We go back to the tepee where they held her," Slocum said, looking at Marlene. She might have blushed. He couldn't tell in the dim light cast by the dying fire. "What they do when we go inside will tell me their plans for us."

"What do you think they'll do?" blurted Marlene.

The brave closest to her lifted his hand to slap her. Slocum moved faster, interposing himself between her and the Blackfoot. The brave glared at him, then put on a poker face.

Slocum and the other two went to the tepee. As they ducked inside, Slocum made a quick survey and found two braves had been stationed close by as guards. They might have been guests of honor at the victory celebration, but they were little more than prisoners now. The Blackfoot had to realize holding three whites was a liability. The skirmish with the Crow showed increasing unrest that would only bring out the cavalry. Whether the Blackfoot wanted the trouble of keeping a white woman as a slave hardly mattered. They would certainly kill the two white men, and might add a woman to their predation without any thought at all.

As he slipped into the tepee, Slocum was almost bowled over when Marlene crashed into him.

"What are we going to do? Are they going to let us go?"

He steered her to the center of the tepee and sat. He motioned for Jackson to join them so he could speak softly enough that the Indians outside couldn't overhear. While he didn't know for certain, he thought the men guarding them spoke enough English to report to the chief anything they overheard.

"Can you find the horses?" Slocum asked Jackson.

"I know where they are corralled."

"You might have to shoot a guard or two. Can you do that?"

"I don't have a pistol." Jackson's eyes widened as Slocum handed over his six-shooter.

"Don't shoot unless you have to. The Blackfoot will be on you like fleas on a dog. If you find a guard, club him. But don't take chances." Slocum glanced in Marlene's direction. She had turned pale again.

"What are you going to do, sir?" Marlene asked.

"I'll distract the two watching us, then create a commotion to decoy them away as you escape."

"How will you get away?" Marlene asked.

Slocum ignored the question. Chances were good that he wouldn't. The more fuss he raised, the better the chance she and the photographer had to get away. He drew his knife.

"I'll give you the sign to go," Slocum said.

"You *do* expect to escape, too, don't you, Mr. Slocum?" Marlene gripped his arm with an intensity that surprised him, considering what she thought about him after finding him searching Leroq's wagon.

"Let him go, Miss Wilkes," the photographer said.

She squeezed a little harder, then pulled back. Slocum came to his feet, walked to the back of the tepee, and found the hole he had cut earlier. He pressed his eye to the hide and looked around, then shoved his blade into the wall and drew it down quickly. He motioned for Marlene and Jackson to exit through the hole. Jackson slid through. Marlene was slower to go. She looked hard at Slocum, started to speak, then followed the photographer.

Slocum went to the door flap, dropped to his hands and knees, and began groaning. He inched forward from the door and poked his head outside. Both Indians came to see what the ruckus was all about. As one bent, Slocum dispatched him with a quick slash. The other responded with the reflexes of a true warrior, his knife coming out and swiping at Slocum.

Rolling, Slocum got away from the deadly knife and came to his feet. He had to end the fight fast. The sound of battle would bring others running. He feinted and moved away slowly. His obvious clumsiness with a knife brought a cry of triumph to the brave's lips. Then the Blackfoot lunged. His knife cut deep into Slocum's left arm.

The next cry from the brave was his last. Slocum had lured him in, committing to the attack that left his belly exposed. Exchanging a minor wound for a death thrust, Slocum stepped back and let the brave collapse to the ground, where his blood pooled with that of his partner.

Wincing as he tied up his wound, Slocum looked around the Blackfoot camp to figure out how best to give Marlene and Jackson a head start. He knew the Blackfoot would give chase as quickly as possible. It was up to him to slow them down.

A quick search of the two dead braves didn't yield him a pistol. Neither had a rifle either. He dragged them into the tepee, then walked boldly into the middle of the settlement. A few fires sputtered. He worked up a torch using a dried limb, then started through the camp applying the flames to every tepee he passed. Within minutes the dried hides had caught and burned with a vengeance.

By the time he had set fire to a half-dozen dwellings, the alarm had been raised. He changed his tactics then and waited for the first brave to rush past him with a rifle. Slocum's knife flashed out, was buried in the man's kidney, twisted about until death descended. With a quick grab, Slocum had a Spencer. He started firing at targets on the far side of the camp. When the rifle came up empty, he used it as a club on another Blackfoot. This time he snatched a six-gun from the brave's waistband.

Slocum never hurried as he worked his way toward the edge of the camp. He picked up another rifle and left behind a corpse. A few shots were necessary to stop braves who had spotted him and knew he was the cause of their woe.

He had no idea if Jackson had found the horses or if he and Marlene were already riding back to the expedition. Jackson might have kept his head and scared off the Blackfoot remuda, though Slocum couldn't count on that.

He drew the pistol and discharged it twice to clear the way from the Blackfoot camp. The fires he had set were almost put out, but the Blackfoot still ran around, shouting and as roused as an anthill with boiling water poured down it. Slocum had a very short time before they began to hunt for the source of their calamity.

A stream of Blackfoot headed toward their horses. In the confusion, Slocum paralleled them, then saw that Jackson had released the remuda, leaving the Indians on foot. That increased Jackson and Marlene's chances of escape. And it doomed Slocum. He had no way of getting away from the Blackfoot camp other than to run.

13

Slocum dropped to his knees when a few braves turned and came in his direction. The darkness saved him. They lightly ran a few yards away, never seeing him in their determination to recover their horses. Slocum saw that the larger group of Indians had gone in a different direction. He went after the trio who had passed him.

As one slowed, Slocum slugged him with his captured pistol and grabbed his rifle. He ran hard to catch up with the other two. One let out a whoop as he spotted a horse and went to retrieve it. The other Blackfoot was slower; Slocum swung the rifle and caught the man on the side of the head. Bonelessly collapsing, the Indian lay without moving. Slocum jumped over the body and brought up the rifle to sight in on the third Blackfoot, now astride his horse.

The brave saw Slocum at the same instant that his trigger finger came back. The rifle bucked and the Indian fell off the horse. The pony reared and pawed at the air, giving Slocum the chance to grab for its reins. If it had bolted and run, he could never have chased it down in the dark. As it was, getting his hand tangled in the reins almost brought about his death by dragging.

The horse tossed its head and shied away, yanking Slocum off his feet. He grabbed with his left hand but could hardly close on the reins. The wound on his left forearm began bleeding again. The horse backed away, keeping Slocum off balance. When he finally got his feet under him, the horse charged.

Slocum had done his share of bronco breaking and had expected the maneuver. Even knowing what the horse was likely to try, he was almost trampled. He got to one side, threw his arms around the horse's neck, and kicked hard. For a moment, he thought he had failed; his toes cut double grooves in the soft earth. Then he found a rock that let him kick out and send himself into the air. He landed hard on the horse's back, his arms still circled its straining neck.

Until he got his bearings, Slocum let the horse run. Even if it tried to gallop through the middle of the Blackfoot encampment, he was better off on the horse than he ever could be without it under him.

Getting his seat, Slocum switched the reins around so he could guide the horse where he desired. He heaved a big sigh. Lady Luck graced him again. Rather than going into the Indian camp, the horse had chosen to run away into the night. Slocum let the horse have its head until it began flagging. He slowed the breakneck pace and eventually got it to a more sedate trot.

The clouds building over the mountains blocked the stars and robbed him of his bearings. He kept riding toward the hulking black outlines of rock, knowing this was leading him westward. When the stars peeked through the clouds, he changed his course and headed toward the North Star. As he rode, he kept a sharp lookout for Blackfoot prowling about intent on revenge. The land was barren of anyone else. After a couple hours, he reached a river pouring down out of the mountains, changed course again, and followed the river, occasionally riding through the water to erase his tracks if the Blackfoot tried to follow him.

Only when he was sure he was somewhere south of where the expedition had stopped days earlier did he leave the river and eventually find the wagons. Slocum drew rein and studied the camp for any sign that the Indians had attacked. The wagons weren't arrayed in a defensive pattern. He didn't know if that was a good sign. The cartographers might be unprepared for an attack.

Slocum rode toward the wagon Hayden used as his office and was relieved to see that the doctor had returned from his survey work. Hayden lay sprawled under his wagon, snoring loudly. He didn't take it kindly when Slocum woke him to deliver his warning about the Blackfoot.

"We can't fight off a war party," Hayden said. "Can we outrun them?" He read the answer on Slocum's face. "What do we do then, sir?"

"Be alert. There's nothing more you can do."

"We can change our destination. I had intended to go east for a week, then turn north. If we break camp tomorrow morning and proceed immediately northward, we might avoid them altogether."

"Keeping the mountains on your flank reduces the ways they can attack, too," Slocum said. "Out in the open on the plains leaves you exposed in all directions."

"I had wanted to avoid some of the rockier terrain. There are more geysers in this direction, too, and our luck might have been exhausted on the mud flats."

"How's Abel? Preston?" Slocum asked.

"Both are doing well."

"And Leroq?"

Hayden frowned, then said, "I cannot say. He was gone when I returned from my mapping. He must have set out to paint."

Slocum wondered if the artist had left the expedition to get the hell away from being revealed as a jewel thief. If the man had stolen a ruby, he might have stolen a great deal more. But where had he hidden Innick's precious gem?

"What of Jackson and his . . . assistant?"

"Haven't seen them. I assumed they were out working, as is Leroq. What do you know of them?"

Slocum hadn't mentioned them, hoping to focus on the threat posed by the Indians. If the photographer and Marlene hadn't reached the camp, they might have been captured. This shouldn't pose any dilemma for Hayden. His duty lay with the greater number of surveyors.

"I'll see to them. You get the expedition on the trail again."

"Very well." Hayden fumbled in his bedroll and found a pocket watch. He flipped open the cover and peered at it. "It's a little past four a.m. If we roll as quickly as possible, we can be a mile away before sunrise."

"Do it," Slocum said. Putting as much distance between the expedition and the Indians was the only way they had of avoiding a fight they could never win. The Blackfoot might settle down after recovering their mounts and go hunting for other Crow war parties. That was their best hope for keeping their scalps in place.

Slocum left Hayden to pulling on his boots and rousing the others. The party responded with ill grace but more speed than Slocum would have thought possible. The threat of possible skirmishing with Indians on the warpath lent speed to their actions.

He went to the darkroom wagon and opened the door. Empty. Jackson and Marlene hadn't returned. He sat on the back step for a few minutes, going over what he knew of the terrain between the expedition camp and that of the Blackfoot. As the other wagons began pulling away, he heaved to his feet, tugged on the reins of his stolen Indian pony, and swung up. Riding bareback wasn't hard, but Slocum wished he had a saddle under him.

From the occasional glimpses of stars through the

gathering storm clouds, he started his search in the direction most likely to cross trails with Jackson and Marlene—if they had escaped at all. Slocum wouldn't allow himself to worry over the chance they had been caught or killed. By an hour after sunrise, he topped an incline and saw them.

Pulling his battered Stetson down to shield his eyes, he carefully studied their back trail. To his relief he saw no hint of pursuit by the Blackfoot or anyone else. He urged the pony down the gentle slope and rode for the spot where the two riders would be in another hour.

"Mr. Slocum!" the photographer cried, waving when he spotted where Slocum had dismounted to await their arrival.

Slocum acknowledged Jackson's greeting but watched Marlene more closely. Her posture improved. She sat straighter and preceded Jackson, reaching Slocum a full minute ahead of her employer.

"You got away," she stated. Her words lacked any emotion.

"I watched your back trail. The Indians didn't follow you, but you left a trail a blind man could find."

"Are we in danger?"

Slocum looked up. The storm had built over the mountains and began spilling out onto the plains.

"Hayden is driving north. We can catch up if we hurry."

"But the Indians, Mr. Slocum," said Jackson, almost out of breath. "Will they come after us? We witnessed the havoc you wrought in their camp." For the first time, Slocum saw the man had managed to hang on to his case of precious photographs. How he had done that was a complete mystery since Slocum knew he hadn't had it when they left the tepee.

Slocum didn't want to find out if Jackson had returned for it—or sent Marlene back into the Blackfoot camp to fetch it.

"Luck might be with us again if it rains. That will wipe out any hoofprints you left and will hide where the expedition went. I doubt they are angry enough to do much more in the way of finding us."

"That's good to hear," Marlene said, slumping again in the saddle.

"You could have taken a couple more horses, other than your own," Slocum said. "That would have made escape easier."

"Ah, yes, ride a horse until it tires, then switch. I am familiar with that technique," Jackson said. "Did you do that to reach Hayden before us?"

"I took what I could." Slocum patted the stolen pony's neck. "My sense of direction is a mite better than yours, I suppose."

"We had to avoid pursuit," Marlene said, testier than before. "You obviously did not have such an obstacle to overcome."

Slocum laughed and shook his head. She would never know.

"Let's ride," he said. "A raindrop just hit my hat brim."

By the time they reached Jackson's darkroom wagon, the downpour had washed away not only the trail dust from their clothing but also their trail.

"The light's too good for me to pass up this chance," William Jackson said, balancing a tripod on one shoulder as he carried a camera and a small wooden case for his photographic plates. "I won't be too long."

"Is it safe?" Marlene asked anxiously.

"Mr. Slocum is sure the Indians did not pursue us in that torrential downpour." Jackson took a deep, appreciative breath and let it out slowly. "The rain has purified the air and turned it crystal clear. I *must* photograph the mountains or turn in my credentials as the foremost photographer in America. It is a pity I lost my best camera outside the Crow camp, but the photographs proved to be spectacular. I must add to my folio, and this shoot will do just that." He shifted his burden, then set out with a long stride and a tune on his lips.

"He will be all right, won't he?" Marlene asked, looking after her employer.

"The Blackfoot band rode east, out onto the plains." Slocum had done a bit of quick scouting. The Blackfoot might be pursuing the Crow. More likely from the way they had moved their entire village, they were hunting for better game and had abandoned their vengeance against both the other Indians and the white men who had so disrupted their life for a few days.

"That's a relief. We will catch up with Dr. Hayden in a day or two?"

"Yeah, if he travels the way he has been, moving, then camping to map for a day or two before moving on," Slocum said. He liked the way she heaved a sigh of relief. Her breasts rose and fell, then bounced just a little.

"I spoke with William on our way back to the wagon, after we escaped the Indian camp," she said, not looking at him. The sunlight slanted down and caught her hair, turning it into a halo that might have glowed from within. Her oval face and bright chocolate eyes were well nigh perfect. Slocum might have seen a more beautiful woman in his day, but right now he couldn't put a name or place to it if he had.

"He said you risked your life to save him, then again to get us out of the Blackfoot camp. The Indians were intent on doing terrible things to me. He said they would have kept me as a slave!"

"Maybe not," Slocum said. She turned on him, her expression flaring toward anger. "They would have used you as a scullery maid for a spell, then let one of the junior members of the tribe marry you. You would have made a good second or third wife."

"What! That's worse! They couldn't! That's not civilized."

"It is for them," Slocum said. "Prisoners taken in battle don't usually fare that well. You'd have made a good squaw."

"Don't be disgusting." Her cheeks colored and her eyes flashed. Then she saw his grin. "You're joshing me. Oh, you!"

Slocum sat on the rear step leading into the darkroom as he watched her pacing about. He knew the signs when a person worked up to a decision. It wouldn't take Marlene long to make up her mind.

"You saved me. Twice. And William. But you're a sneak thief. You tried to rob Gustav."

"Fact is," Slocum said, "that peacock is the thief. I worked for a man by the name of Sean Innick out by Otter Creek in Utah. A thief stole all his wife's jewelry. I caught the thief and turned him over the marshal, but a big ruby was missing. It'd been in Mrs. Innick's family for a spell, and she wants to give it as a wedding gift to her daughter next month."

"But you said you caught the thief."

"Leroq hired the thief. The robber said he gave the stone to Leroq. I promised to fetch it back before the wedding so's not to disappoint Mrs. Innick or her daughter." He didn't bother her with his momentarily wrong notion that Jackson might have been the one who had hired the thief. That would only muddy the waters.

"That . . . that's rather noble."

"You caught me hunting for it. I haven't had a chance to find out firsthand from Leroq what he did with it."

"You wouldn't have found it unless . . ."

"Unless what?" Slocum's sharp tone caused her to jump as if he had snapped a whip.

"There's no way you could know since you aren't an artist."

"He didn't have the ruby. I need to find where he stashed it."

"Did you find a mortar and pestle?"

Slocum rubbed his fingers together as he remembered the gritty feel on the mortar.

"Yes, you did. That grit you felt was the ruby. Did you find a jar of red dust?"

"What was it?" Slocum asked suspiciously.

"Gustav smashed the ruby, then used the mortar and pestle to grind it into dust."

"The ruby's gone? Except the red dust?" Slocum felt as if he had stepped off a cliff. The five-hundred-dollar reward had just evaporated. "Why'd he go and do a thing like that? A dandy like him, I'd expect him to mount it to a stickpin and flash it around with his fancy clothing and all."

"Artists have put odd things into their paint for years— for centuries. El Greco used ground-up emeralds in his paint. When the picture was completed, the light reflected off it in a way unlike any other artist's work. There was a distinctive hue, a look, a feel. Gustav uses rubies."

"Ground-up rubies," Slocum said. "What am I going to tell Mrs. Innick?"

"You would return to tell her?"

"Of course I would," Slocum said. "I gave my word."

Marlene came closer, her skirts whispering as she moved across the damp grass. She stopped a foot away from him.

"I misjudged you terribly. I am sorry."

"You didn't know the facts."

"I do now. You're a very brave man, one who risked his life for me, one who wants to do right by a woman and her daughter who's getting married." Marlene moved even closer, then dropped to her knees in front of where he sat on the lower step.

She reached out and worked at the buttons on his fly.

"Let me apologize."

"You don't have to," Slocum said, but his words were at odds with what he felt as her feathery touch caressed his organ and her hot breath gusted around his crotch to excite him.

Her lips touched the tip, then sucked gently to draw his limp length into her mouth. He didn't stay limp long. Her eager tongue swirled and stroked until he was steely hard in her mouth. Then she began moving back and forth with a tormentingly slow motion that went from the purpled knob on the end of his cock all the way down until she had him entirely in her mouth.

She backed away, pushing him out with her tongue. Her lips kissed and caressed, then she moved back to take him fully again. This time she turned her head slightly so his manhood rubbed across her soft inner cheek. As she moved with more determination, her lips tightened in a firm, warm circle around him. He moaned and leaned back, elbows on the next step up.

"That's about the finest I've felt in a while," he said.

She mumbled something around the thick plug in her mouth, then began moving faster, her head bouncing to and fro. Her fingers worked into his jeans and stroked over his hairy balls, pressing and massaging and teasing until he tensed up. The pressures built within his loins. He felt the hot tides mounting, but he wanted more.

Her tongue cradled the sensitive underside of his length. She combined all her ways of stimulation. Her cheeks went hollow as she sucked. Her tongue massaged and stroked across the sensitive head. Her fingers tightened around his balls, and then she tugged as she sucked. The coordinated effort was more than Slocum could withstand.

He exploded like one of the geysers. She rode him, drained him of every drop, until he began to melt in her hot mouth. Marlene rocked back on her heels and looked up at him with a wicked expression. Her tongue slipped between her red lips as she snared a tiny white drop at the corner of her mouth.

"You're tasty," she said.

"That was—" Slocum stood suddenly and began tucking himself back into his jeans. He reached for the Colt slung in his holster—Jackson had escaped the Blackfoot without having to fire it and had been glad to return it to Slocum.

"What is it?" She struggled to her feet and stood at his side.

"I saw movement out there." Slocum pushed her behind him, hardly noticing the flare of pain in his left forearm.

"Oh, it's only William. That didn't take him long," she said. In a low voice she said, "Perhaps we can convince him to go take more photos?"

"Mr. Slocum, Mr. Slocum!" Jackson hurried over, juggling his equipment like a circus performer. He never quite dropped any of it, though he came close in his haste.

"What is it, William?" Marlene stepped away from Slocum.

"It's Gustav. Gustav Leroq!"

"What about him?" Slocum demanded.

"His wagon's not a mile from here, abandoned. He wasn't anywhere to be seen!"

Slocum mounted and rode, following Jackson's tracks easily in the soft ground. If Leroq was dead, Slocum would never know for certain if he had destroyed the ruby—or if he had hidden it somewhere so cleverly that Slocum had missed it in his earlier search.

14

It took Slocum less than fifteen minutes to spot Leroq's wagon pulled down into a ravine. From the look of it, the wagon had been parked there before the prior day's rains. He circled the area hunting for tracks, but the rain that had erased any trace of a trail for the Blackfoot had also erased tracks Slocum might follow to find Gustav Leroq.

He dismounted and fastened his pony's reins to the rear wagon wheel. He climbed into the wagon bed, intending to hunt once more for the ruby. He didn't doubt Marlene when she said Leroq might have destroyed the ruby, but he had to be sure. The glass jar with the red powder in it was on top of the box with the rest of Leroq's paints. Slocum pulled the cork and rubbed the powder between his fingers again. The grit might be from ground-up ruby. The sunlight glinted off the dust in the jar in a way that bedazzled.

He grunted. That was what Marlene had said. The ground ruby mixed with paint caused a special reflection in a drawing. Like a watermark. This glint certified the painting was a Leroq original. Slocum recorked the jar and dropped it back into the paint box. If that was Innick's ruby, there wasn't any point in returning the powder to the sawmill owner.

Slocum made his way to the back of the wagon. As he started to jump down, he noticed that one of the fancy crates Dillingham had made for Leroq was out of place. He turned it around, then opened it. Inside rested two canvases on frames that hadn't been there before. Heaving one up, he matched the scene with that on the other side of the mountain pass where Slocum had rescued the artist from the Blackfoot hunting party. He dropped it back into its slot and looked at the other.

Turning to face the mountains, he matched this scene with the one Jackson had been so eager to photograph. While he couldn't tell how long ago Leroq had painted the picture, it couldn't have been too long. Slocum pressed his thumb into one corner. He left a fingerprint in the still tacky paint. When he held the thumb up to the sunlight, the paint glinted with a subdued reddish hue. Leroq had painted this using Innick's ruby.

Slocum stuck the painting back into the case and closed the lid. From his position in the wagon, he slowly turned in a full circle to catch any sight of Leroq. The rain had wiped out any tracks, and the artist must have been ridden away on one of his team the day before, since one horse remained. Slocum stared at the mountains, envisioning the scene that artist had painted.

"Where else would he paint if he'd already done this view?" Slocum asked himself.

He wasn't an artist. There didn't seem to be any other scenic view that would appeal to a man who had a month or more of travel ahead of him. From what Slocum remembered of Yellowstone, there were far more breathtaking views of waterfalls and vistas from mountaintops. Leroq wouldn't waste time here when he could preserve his paint and canvas for later in the exploration.

Where would he go? Slocum turned away from the

mountains and looked toward the east. He saw no reason why Leroq would ride that way. Hayden intended to move north; to the west, the mountains blocked travel, and Leroq had already come from the south.

Slocum stepped from the wagon to horseback and trotted north, the only direction that made sense for Leroq to travel. Less than an hour later, he came upon a small town set in a shallow bowl on the plains. He caught his breath. He had thought they were farther from civilization than this.

Marlene had probably been right when she said Leroq had ground up the ruby. Everything Slocum had found—or not found—in the artist's wagon supported that. Still, he had to know. If nothing else, he would take Leroq back to Marshal Smith, though what good that did anyone was a puzzle. Putting Leroq in jail for the theft did nothing to get the precious stone back.

As Slocum rode slowly down the main street, he felt all eyes on him. There was only one road leading into town, coming from the south, and he was on it. Nothing from any other direction. This was an outpost, maybe supplying the local ranches. Strangers in this area had to stand out like a sore thumb.

He went into the lone saloon and went to the bar. The wall-eyed woman canted her head to one side and asked, "Who you want?"

Slocum tried not to show surprise as he answered, "A dandy named Leroq. He rode this way in the last day or two."

"You and ever' single gunslinger in the county."

"Do tell." Slocum indicated he wanted a beer. Whiskey would have been good, but he needed more than a single shot sliding down his gullet. It had been a long, thirsty ride to find yet another place where Leroq had gotten himself into hot water.

She dropped a mug in front of him. Slocum nodded in appreciation when he felt the cold mug. Cold beer went down a sight better than warm. He drained it, then asked, "What trouble's he in?"

"Stole a tinhorn gambler's stickpin. A fine headlight diamond worth a thousand dollars."

"Or so said the gambler," Slocum concluded. He didn't get any argument. "Anyone see him swipe it?"

"Who else? He was the only stranger in town." She closed one eye and studied him. "You a bounty hunter after that flashy dude?"

Slocum said nothing. Being named a bounty hunter irritated him, but he realized that stood him in good stead. He didn't have to explain why he wanted Leroq.

"You got some competition. The gambler fellow hired himself a couple cowboys from the Lazy T to fetch him back and hang him."

"The gambler offer a reward for the diamond?" Slocum wondered how much had been offered. Two empty beer mugs had to be his limit if he wanted to stay sharp. There might be another reward in the offing.

"Can't say, but them boys was mighty eager to get on the dandy's trail."

"Thanks," he said, dropping a dime on the bar to pay for the beers. It felt good having a roll of bank notes in his pocket but he wasn't likely to get much in return for paper money issued by a Salt Lake City bank.

He stepped out and felt eyes on him again. It wouldn't do much good to ask after Leroq, not with locals already on his trail. Another outsider only took the bounty money away from the town. The cowboys were locals and would spend their reward at the saloon, at stores, at the local whorehouse.

Slocum took the time to go to a saddle shop and dicker awhile to buy a new saddle and gear. If he had to ride, using stirrups was better than doing it bareback. Along with this he stopped at the general store and bought some victuals for the trail. Only then did he concentrate on his real mission.

There was no reason for Leroq to ride east or west. Slocum had come from the south and hadn't seen him. That meant the artist had gone north. He mounted up, appreciating the feel of a leather saddle under him once more, and rode in that direction. As he left town, he watched the people whisper and point. From their reaction he knew he had again read Leroq's intention well. The man was hunting for scenic territory to paint and wasn't going to find it anywhere around this town.

He reached the rim of the bowl holding the town and stared at the horizon. Too much land to search. He angled to the northwest. The only place he knew Leroq would return to was the wagon. He might cut off the artist on his way back. A half-day's ride brought two men into view. Both walked their horses, staring at the ground as if following a trail.

Slocum turned slowly to see where the tracks led, then caught his breath. He let it out in a huge rush along with curses that turned the air blue. Leroq had been nothing but trouble for him, and the artist continued to rack up new ways to involve Slocum in matters he would rather avoid.

The trackers were less than a hundred yards from where Leroq lounged, his back propped up by the gentle rise that hid him from direct view of the two cowboys. The artist stared up at the empty sky rather than worrying about men hunting for him. Slocum judged distances and knew he could never reach Leroq before the cowboys stumbled across their quarry. If he took a potshot at them to draw their attention, he stood a chance of getting shot off his horse. Explaining how he rode a captured Blackfoot pony wasn't in the cards.

He headed straight for Leroq, hoping the man noticed and hightailed it. If Slocum could get between the artist and his pursuers, he might talk them out of leaving his carcass out on the plains for hungry buzzards.

Halfway there, Slocum saw that he was too late. The cowboys walked over the rise and spotted Leroq immediately. They slapped leather and got their six-shooters out, trained on the dandy in his faded purple jacket and torn silk pants. That they didn't gun him down out of hand gave

Slocum some small hope. He galloped toward them in time to hear one cowboy saying, "You tell us where it is or die right here, on this very spot."

"Good work, men," Slocum shouted. He kept riding, taking advantage of the surprised cowboys. "You caught him fair and square. Can I ride with you as you take him back to town?"

"Who the hell are you?"

"Another bounty hunter," Slocum said. The lie came easier now that he spoke it.

"But you're—" Leroq began.

"From Otter Creek, over in Utah. He stole some jewelry there."

"Kept up his crime spree, he did," the other cowboy said. He looked at his partner. "We ain't sharin' the reward fer this owlhoot."

"Not asking for that," Slocum said. "Just want to make sure he stays alive so I can send a telegram back to Marshal Smith."

"Telegram?" The two men laughed. "No telegraph in Sulfur Springs."

"Well, I'll ride along anyway."

"Slocum, you—" Leroq clamped his mouth shut when he saw Slocum's black look.

"He have the diamond on him?" Slocum asked.

"We was just startin' to inquire." The two cowboys stripped Leroq down to his underclothing. Slocum wasn't surprised to see those were silk, too.

What the two men didn't find was the diamond.

"Where'd you put it, you flea-bit dog?" One cowboy brought his six-gun up to buffalo Leroq.

"Not the way to get him to tell you," Slocum said. The cowboy jerked around, angry. He stared down the barrel of Slocum's Colt.

Not for the first time, Slocum considered taking out the two cowboys and making Leroq talk. He had been denied such a talk since joining the expedition. If Leroq hadn't been drunk, he had been in a coma. Slocum wanted to find out for certain that the ruby was gone. What he would do then was something he had to work on. Letting these two kill Leroq wasn't in the cards.

"We caught him," one man said sullenly.

"Let's get him back to town. Sulfur Springs, you called it?"

"Ain't got a lawman."

"There's somewhere to lock him up until a trial. There must be."

"Trial?" Both cowboys stared at Slocum as if he had grown a second head.

"That's the way the law works. Mount up," Slocum said to Leroq. The arrogant artist was clever enough to realize how close he was to dying, and only Slocum stood between him and a few lead slugs ventilating him.

Slocum and Leroq rode ahead of the two cowboys. This made Slocum a tad edgy since those men were interested only in the reward, not bringing in a prisoner. If it took shooting Slocum in the back as well, they would. A quick glance backward now and they kept their hands away from their six-guns. For how long, Slocum didn't know.

"Talk fast," he said to Leroq. "Did you steal Sean Innick's ruby?"

"I stole nothing!"

"Did you have a robber you found in Otter Creek steal the jewelry and did you keep the ruby?"

"I, uh, the word 'have' is a bit strong."

"What happened to the ruby?"

Leroq rode, stewing, before he finally said, "I ground it up."

"To put in your paint," Slocum said. He felt a burden lifted from his shoulders. He hadn't failed to find the gem— it had been the jar of dust. What he would do now was a matter of conscience.

Returning the stone was impossible. That meant he wouldn't get the extra five-hundred-dollar reward. Was there anything to be gained hauling Leroq to jail?

"Did you already grind up the diamond, too?" Slocum asked.

Leroq looked at him in surprise. His mouth opened but no words came out. He closed his mouth, then said, "I know nothing of any diamond. Why would I care to have a diamond? There's no way to grind it up. It's too obdurate."

"You mean it's too hard?"

"A very difficult gemstone, sir, not like emerald or ruby or other stones that lend distinctive color and texture to an oil."

"Oil?"

"My paint, dammit, you buffoon!"

Slocum considered what Leroq had said, and it carried an undercurrent of truth to it. Leroq saw nothing wrong in stealing a stone to put into his paint since it was for art. If he couldn't use it, he didn't take it. The way he had given the gold jewelry to the actual thief back in Otter Creek showed that.

"What happened to the diamond?"

"What diamond is that?" Leroq frowned. "I saw a gambler with a headlight diamond, a stickpin of some size. He plied his abominable trade in the drinking establishment in that nothing of a town. Is that the diamond to which you refer?"

"The gambler claims you swiped it. What dealings did you have with him?"

"I spoke with him at some length about the diamond and other precious stones, that's all. He was a bit soused. Pickled! But I did not steal his diamond. There was no reason to. I am engaged in creation, in the throes of genius as I find inspiration in the beauty of this land."

Slocum ignored most of Leroq's fine speech. He didn't know why he believed the artist about the current theft, but he did. Someone else around Sulfur Springs must have stolen the diamond. Without more facts, Slocum had no idea who that might be.

"You cannot allow me to be detained here, Slocum. Dr. Hayden needs my services. Who else can capture the grandeur of this unique country?"

"Jackson takes photographs that look exactly like the land."

"He is a photographer, not a true artist who captures the vitality, the *soul* of the countryside. Hayden will be useless without me. His expedition will be soulless. All he will return to Washington are flat maps with no character whatsoever."

"We kin lock the son of a bitch up in the back of the saloon till the trial," one cowboy said loudly.

"Real good idea, Ike. Betty Sue won't mind. She kin look the other way!"

This produced gales of laughter. Slocum knew that Betty Sue was the wall-eyed barkeep and maybe the saloon owner.

"You must save me from these dastards!" Leroq implored Slocum.

"Only way to keep you from dancing at the end of a rope is find who stole the diamond."

Leroq sputtered as the two cowboys led him into the saloon. Slocum dismounted and followed them inside, wondering how long he had to find the real thief before the good people of Sulfur Springs hung Leroq.

Not long was his guess. Not long at all.

15

"Where'd the gambler get off to?" Slocum asked Betty Sue. The woman peered at him out of the eye going off in its own direction.

"Sam's usually drunker 'n a skunk this time of day. 'Bout cleaned out. He met up with a cowboy what knowed odds better 'n him, at least whilst he's snockered."

"Where is he?"

"He ain't offerin' no reward, that's for sure, not 'less he gets that fancy diamond of his back. He don't trust banks any more 'n the rest of us. That's how he carries his money from the good times, so's he can sell it to tide him over. Now he ain't got nuthin'."

"Let me have a bottle," Slocum said. This surprised the barkeep, but she dutifully put it on the bar. "There a boardinghouse where Sam's likely to be?"

"Down the street thataways," Betty Sue said, pointing. She clasped her hands together. "You won't find him, though. He's . . . somewhere else."

Slocum paid for the popskull and left. Small towns were closemouthed about prattle, unless you lived there. In that case, the gossip was nonstop. He hadn't seen a hotel any-where. That reduced the number of spots where a gambler might hang his hat at night. He had no trouble finding what had to be the only boardinghouse in town. On the front porch, rocked back in a chair, hat pulled down, and snoring like a ripsaw working through hard wood, a man dressed as a gambler mumbled and thrashed about. Sitting beside him, Slocum pulled out the cork with a loud pop, then waved the open whiskey bottle under the man's nose.

The huge nose twitched. Then he sneezed and his eyes came open. There might have been more than one man on a week-long bender, but if so, their eyes couldn't have been more bloodshot.

"Take a pull," Slocum said.

"Thanks, mister." Sam sucked up a swallow of liquor, then took another for good measure. "I know you?"

"Nope," Slocum said, "but I'm the man who's going to get your stickpin back."

"My diamond!" The transformation was immediate. The gambler had gone from drunk and hungover to alert in a trice. "You got it back?"

"I can," Slocum said. "They got a fellow locked up over at the saloon, but he didn't steal it."

"The fancy-ass-dressed stranger? He musta been the one."

"Take my word for it. He didn't steal it. Tell me what you remember."

"I was just cleaned out at the table. Damned fool thing to do, holdin' two low pair when I knowed he had three of a kind. I could see it in his eyes, but he had bluffed before. Not too good. Thought he was doin' it again."

"You know the player?"

"Gerald Prood, the foreman out on the Lazy T. That's a spread up north o' here. Not the biggest, but it's a good one. I shoulda took my loss but I bet ever'thing."

And lost.

"Three kings. Prood had three kings. All I had was fours and sixes."

"What then?"

"He bought me a drink." Sam clutched the bottle Slocum had given him like it was the most precious thing in the world. When Slocum indicated he could take another swig, Sam did. His throat lubricated, he said, "Bought me several. He helped me out of the saloon but I started to get all queasy, so he left me in a chair outside to puke out my guts. I did."

Slocum encouraged the gambler to keep talking.

"That dude come out of the saloon. I seen him earlier and tried to get him into a game. Said he didn't play poker. 'Magine that. Not play poker. Asked if I needed help. Stood me up and walked me around a bit. When I got my legs under me, he went on his way."

"And that's when you noticed the diamond was gone."

"I went damned near loco hunting for it in the dirt. Even pawed through my own puke. Had to be him what stole it."

"You have it when Prood helped you out?"

"Surely did."

"Did you have it when Prood left you?"

"Must have."

Slocum did some quick figuring and knew what had happened to the diamond, but a man who was foreman on a good ranch hardly seemed the kind to steal the diamond, especially when he had just won the gambler's entire poke.

"Good boy, Gerald Prood. He's gettin' married real soon. Soon as he convinces the boss to let his daughter marry a hired hand." Sam hiccoughed and looked wistfully at the bottle.

"You keep that safe for me. We can have a celebration drink when I come back with your diamond."

"You gonna get it from that fancy-dressin' dude?"

Slocum let Sam begin the celebration on his own. He knew about everything he needed. All he had to do was prove it to get Leroq out of Sulfur Springs before they lynched him.

Finding the road out to the Lazy T was easy enough. It was well traveled, but Slocum had no idea what to say when he got there. The ranch house was painted and in good repair. Slocum rode up and tipped his hat to the young woman on the front porch.

"Ma'am, can you tell me where to find Gerald Prood?"

"Who's calling for him?" She was a tiny thing, like a porcelain doll, but her question carried the snap of command. She was used to giving orders and having them obeyed.

"Got an important message. Seems he has come into some money."

"You may leave it with me. I'm his fiancée." She lowered her voice and looked around as if she might have been overheard. This confirmed Slocum's suspicions. Prood and the young woman intended to marry but had yet to get permission from her pa.

"Can't do that," Slocum said. "Tell Gerald he can come into Sulfur Springs in the next day or two. I'm camped outside at the west end of town. If he doesn't show up, I have to ride on."

"But the money."

"Goes to the next one on the list."

"What list?"

"Ma'am, have a good day." Slocum touched the brim of his hat but took a few extra seconds to wheel around to leave. He had her pegged exactly.

"Wait, Gerald's out near the springs north of here. Not a mile out, tending stock. He has to keep them from drinking from the sulfur ponds."

Slocum rode out. He wasn't pleased with himself deceiving the woman into thinking Prood had come into money— but the truth was, the cowboy had. He had won it fair and square from the gambler. What had tempted an otherwise honest man was the sight of the diamond stickpin. That would make one mighty fine engagement ring, sure to impress his boss—the woman's pa.

The stench of sulfur made Slocum sneeze. He rode into a field festooned with small ponds ringed with bright yellow crystalline sulfur. The water bubbled up from underground, not quite boiling but too hot to drink, even without the noxious sulfur in it. When he spotted a manmade stock pond, he knew where to find Prood.

The cowboy herded a dozen head through a narrow gap in the waist-high earthen wall to a broad, shallow pond lacking any hint of the sulfur contaminating the other pools.

Prood jumped when Slocum called to him. The cowboy didn't wear a side arm but had a rifle sheathed at his right leg. The stock pointed backward, telling Slocum that Prood made his way through heavy undergrowth, though where on the grassy plains this might be, he couldn't say.

Might be Prood came from a part of the country where this was a concern.

"Who might you be? How'd you know my name?" Prood leaned back, inching toward the rifle to get it out if the need arose.

"It's one thing to beat a gambler at his own game. That's even admirable," Slocum said. "It's not so admirable to steal his diamond stickpin."

Prood started to draw the rifle. Slocum was quicker. He had his Colt out of the cross-draw holster, cocked, and aimed before the cowboy could get a good grip on his rifle.

"You stole Sam's diamond. I met your intended. Lovely girl, but she doesn't need a diamond to make her marry you."

"Her pa—"

"Her pa wants the best for her, 'less I miss my guess. That's not a man who steals. Win all the poker pots you can, but don't rob a man who's too drunk to stand up."

"Some'd say gambling with a drunk and taking his money that way's no different."

"Well, Gerald," Slocum said, "some fools might say that. If a man—a gambler who makes his living off cards—can't stay sober enough at the table, that's his problem. If you'd matched him pennies for the diamond and he'd lost, that would be his problem too. Only that's not the way it happened. You took it when he was puking out his guts."

"I . . . it caught on my sleeve. I didn't notice till later and—"

"Your girl's not likely to ever marry a liar either."

"What do you want from me?"

Slocum considered the situation, then came to a decision.

"We're going back to Sulfur Springs."

Gerald Prood slumped and nodded in defeat.

"Go on," Slocum urged. "Tell them all what happened. Just like you told me out on the trail."

Prood had gone pale under his tanned, weather-beaten face. He reached into his coat pocket and brought out the diamond. Hand shaking, he put it on the bar.

"Thass my stickpin!" Sam reached for it then hesitated, looking up at Prood. "How'd you come by it?"

"He found it, Sam," Slocum said. "Go on, Gerald. Tell them. Just like you told me on the way to town."

Everything Prood said was almost the truth. It was the complete truth if "found" and "stole" were the same thing. As he started talking, Slocum ordered drinks for the house. By the time Gerald had finished his tale of finding the stone, putting it away for safekeeping and only now returning it because he'd had powerful important chores to do at the Lazy T, most everyone in the saloon believed him.

Slocum saw that Betty Sue remained skeptical, but Sam's enthusiasm for getting his property back dimmed any questions she might have. With another round for the house lubricating everyone's good sense and causing it to slip a mite, no one questioned Gerald about his lapse.

No one except Betty Sue.

"What took you away in such a hurry, Gerald?" she asked. "Cain't fer the life of me imagine what that might be."

"I . . . I had to ride home to propose to Miss Dunlap."

"And she said yes," Slocum said.

The cheers drowned out any other question the barkeep might have. If Slocum could tell, she was convinced this was what had happened, and any thought of Prood being a sneak thief vanished in the joy. A wedding in a town like Sulfur Springs had to be quite an event. Other than funerals and births, there was little else here to get folks together.

"You figure you can let Leroq out of the back room now?" Slocum asked.

Betty Sue looked as if she'd bit down on a lemon, then nodded.

"I was hopin' fer a necktie party to break the boredom."

"A wedding's better," Slocum assured her.

"Is," she agreed. "But Mr. Dunlap's not heard squat about his daughter's nuptials, now has he?"

"It'll work out," Slocum said. He followed her to the padlocked door leading to the storage room.

She worked at the rusty lock until it grated open. Slocum pushed past into the darkened room and almost laughed. Leroq huddled in one corner, filthy and looking like he'd had to shoot and eat his own dog. His hands and feet were securely bound. Slocum used his knife to make quick work of the ropes.

"Come on, we're going back to the expedition," he said.

"Th-They're letting me go?"

"They sure thought you were the one who stole that diamond. A good thing an honest cowboy found it and brought it back."

"Found?"

"Come on," Slocum said, pulling Leroq behind him.

They stepped into the brightly lit saloon. Leroq shielded his eyes, then started for the bottle making its way up and down the bar. Slocum yanked his arm to get him out of the saloon.

"I demand a drink. After all the humiliation heaped upon my head, that is the least that's owed me!"

"Don't give these folks a second more to think about what's happened."

"He didn't confess to stealing the diamond on his own, did he? You coerced him."

"He *found* the diamond. Let it go, Leroq." Slocum got the man into the street. It took a while to find Leroq's horse.

On the trail Leroq said, "It is a pity he didn't have a ruby or emerald. I could have used that to bestow a masterpiece on the world. It would have been a thing of beauty for all time."

"You want crystals to put into your paint?"

"I am always searching."

Slocum rode north out of town, then angled to the west, following the stench of sulfur to a string of small geysers.

"There," Slocum said. "Use some of that."

"Sulfur? Don't be absurd, Slocum. My paintings will never smell of gunpowder. Besides, the ground crystals become too powdery and lack substance."

"I didn't mean the sulfur," Slocum said, stepping down. He went to the edge of a bubbling pool, knelt, and pried loose a long purple crystal from the mud. He held it up for Leroq to see. "This."

"Why, that is amethyst."

"Hard enough?" Slocum tapped it with his gun barrel. "Looks to be. Got a distinctive color."

"Purple. Why, royal purple is my favorite color." Leroq tried to preen, to show off his fancy velvet jacket. It now hung in tatters and carried more grime than cloth. Wash it and the coat would vanish.

"If you use this, you can brag on how it comes from the

very scenes you're painting. Gives whoever looks at your paintings the feel of being here." Slocum's nose wrinkled at the sulfur stench. That would be a better reminder of the land than the amethyst.

"Why, yes, that is so. I am glad I have found this." Leroq began gathering as much of the slender purple crystals as he could scoop up.

"And you won't have to do any more stealing, of rubies or emeralds or anything else now?"

"Why, this will last me for months! For a hundred paintings!"

Slocum doubted that, but he had to be content that Leroq wasn't inclined to go hunting for more jewels to steal.

That settled, Slocum was anxious to return to the expedition. And Marlene Wilkes.

16

"It will be good to return to the expedition," Gustav Leroq said. "I am filthy, need new clothing, and my hands shake. They simply shake from lack of work! I must paint. Surrounded by such glory, I must capture it on canvas!"

Slocum ignored the popinjay. Leroq had alternated between sullen and so obnoxiously friendly that he found himself preferring the morose artist to the outgoing one. He had an added annoyance in misjudging where the expedition would be. He had returned to the spot where he thought he had left Marlene and the darkroom wagon and had found nothing. Tracks that should have given him a clue had been erased in one of the frequent, intense, but brief afternoon storms. Not finding the old camp or the tracks to a new one, he had wandered about for two whole days searching. Leroq had come to think of him as an expert in the wilderness, but Slocum wanted the trail to end.

He wanted the trail to end wherever Marlene camped.

"We will return soon. I had no idea I had journeyed so far away to that horrid town."

"You had," Slocum said, looking for a hill where he might get some added distance for his hunt.

"I intended only to drop by for a drink. I had such a thirst after traveling as I had. There wasn't even a decent place for me to paint." He patted the equipment slung on his horse. Leroq had an easel and a box of paints.

"What were you going to paint on? I don't see any canvas or paper."

"Carefully rolled and stored with the easel. I have become quite expert in such matters, having been on a prior expedition into the Dakota Badlands. A terrible place, the Badlands. Filled with Indians not unlike those who badgered me."

"You dealt with the Sioux," Slocum said. "These were Blackfoot." It occurred to him that Leroq knew nothing about the encounter with the Crow. If Jackson or Marlene wanted to tell the story, they could. Slocum found himself too engrossed in finding Hayden and the others.

He almost let out a whoop of glee. Restraining himself made it appear he had led Leroq directly back to the expedition. They had camped beside a small river fed by spring runoff from the mountains to the west. From the look of it, they had been there only a day at the most.

Leroq blithered on; Slocum ignored him.

"Why look, there is my wagon. Someone drove it here for me. I trust they did not harm the paintings."

Slocum looked at his thumb. The paint he had smeared there had long since wiped off. He wondered if Leroq would even notice. The artist galloped ahead. Slocum held back. His horse had put many miles under its hooves the past week, and giving it a bit of a rest would go a long way toward restoring its speed and stamina.

He looked around for Jackson's wagon but didn't see it. Frowning, he hunted for Hayden. He couldn't find the expedition leader either. Rather than guess what had happened, he dismounted and went to Fenwicke. The man stood over a table with rocks holding down an elaborate map dotted with contour lines.

"Ah, Mr. Slocum, you have returned. Just in time, too."

"Where's Hayden?"

"He and Mr. Jackson set off to map early yesterday morning and have not returned."

"When do you expect them back?" His heart sank. Marlene wouldn't be in camp if Jackson had taken his wagon.

"That is something of a mystery. What I mean is, Dr. Hayden did not inform me of his plans. Rather, he left me to complete the detailed map surveyed over the past few miles and all the way to the mountains. We are getting deeper into the territory known as Yellowstone, and none of it has been properly surveyed."

"Until now," Slocum said, hoping to speed along the man's recitation.

"Yes, quite. That's true. I intend to move out in another day or two if the good doctor has not returned. We must keep to schedule, and I daresay we are falling behind because of all that unpleasantness with the Indians."

"The Blackfoot and Crow? Or has there been something more?"

"What? Oh, no, nothing more. We have hurried along to leave that behind, but carelessness has crept in. That's why I must tend to the details Dr. Hayden is glossing over." Fenwicke muttered to himself as he inked in lines on the map.

In disgust, Slocum left and went to find anyone else who knew Hayden's intentions. There were two other scouts, though he'd had no contact with them. If either was in camp, he could learn of the terrain to the north.

"John! John!"

He turned and found his arms filled with a delightfully warm, wiggling Marlene Wilkes. She clung to him with a ferocity that warned him something wasn't right.

"They haven't come back. William said they'd be gone

only a few hours, that they'd be back before sundown. He left me while he took the wagon."

"We've got a couple hours till then," Slocum said. He didn't mind the way she pressed against him. He wished she would release the death lock on his neck, though.

"No, it was *yesterday* before sundown—William said they'd be back by then. I'm so worried!"

"Fenwicke said nothing about them being overdue. If anything, he thought it was to be expected."

"William never takes longer."

Slocum pried her loose. There was always a first time for a photographer—for an artist—to become too engrossed in his work and lose track of time. Instead he said, "Hayden might have needed his help. Fenwicke said both scouts went with them."

"They were back yesterday after dark. I saw them skulking about and tried to get them to tell me where William and Dr. Hayden were. They packed their gear and left."

"There aren't any scouts left?"

"Only you, John. You have to find William. And the doctor."

He had fetched Leroq and brought him back. Why he had bothered after finding the ruby would never be recovered posed something of a problem for him. He ought to have left the man in Sulfur Springs to be hanged for robbery. It was about what he deserved. Only Slocum couldn't do that since Leroq had been innocent of that crime.

That crime. He was guilty as sin of stealing Innick's ruby.

"John, listen to me," she said, gripping his arms. He winced when she squeezed down on his forearm. It was still healing slowly from the knife wound. Marlene was so distraught she never noticed him flinch.

"I'll go after them. I need some clue where to begin hunting. The rains over the past few days have wiped out any tracks they might have left, even driving the darkroom wagon."

"You'll find them faster because William took it. It has to stand out more, be visible, easy to spot."

"Is there any map of the region, no matter how crude, that Hayden might have used?"

"I don't think so. If there is one, Fenwicke has it." Her obvious disgust with the man made her spit out his name as if it burned her tongue.

"Let's see what he can tell us."

Slocum and Marlene garnered more than passing looks as they went to Fenwicke's wagon because of the way they walked, pressed together like leaves between the pages of a Bible. It wouldn't do the woman's reputation any good, but she was oblivious to anything but finding her employer.

Fenwicke didn't even glance up as they approached. He made dismissive motions with his hand, as if he were brushing dirt off his clothing.

"Do leave me alone. This is a more difficult geosyncline structure than I anticipated, though it is not along a coastal region, of course. Rather it is a buildup of volcanic products from the activity throughout the region, causing—"

"A map," Slocum said, loudly enough to bring Fenwicke out of his reverie. "Where Hayden and Jackson were going. Is there any kind of a map?"

"Why, I don't know. If there was, they would have taken it with them."

"Dr. Fenwicke," Marlene said. "This is the region we just passed through, isn't it?"

"Why, of course it is, my dear. You see here—"

"Are the next dozen miles likely to be an extension of this? With the land sloping in this fashion?"

"That is an excellent assumption. You see—"

Marlene led Slocum away as the cartographer mumbled to himself.

"I can sketch a map for you, assuming the volcanic nature of the land to the north isn't too different."

"I'll saddle up and get ready."

"I want to go, too," she said.

"If anything's happened to them, you don't want to get mixed up in it."

"I survived Blackfoot captivity," she said haughtily. "I can survive anything. This is for William. I owe him that much."

"Stay here. I'll find them both and be back safe and sound within a day or two, depending on how far they rode."

The set of the woman's chin told him argument would be futile.

"You won't give me the map, will you? If I don't have it, I can't hunt for them."

"I'll go by myself. Or you can come with me," she said. She crossed her arms and lifted her chin. Slocum had seen determination before, but it paled in the face of Marlene's resolve.

"I can come with *you*?" Slocum had to grin at that. "Saddle up. I don't know how long we're going to be gone."

"Very well, sir," she said. Marlene turned, then half turned and looked back. "What should I pack?"

Slocum laughed outright at that. The flash of aggravation disappeared and she laughed, too.

In a half hour they were riding side by side, going deeper into the volcanically active territory. Slocum proceeded slowly, trying to guess where Hayden would have gone. On horseback, the cartographer would choose a different track than William Jackson with his darkroom wagon. Would they have parted company and gone their separate ways?

"Higher elevations," Slocum said. "Both of them would hunt for a place to look down over the countryside to get the best view."

"A surveyor works in all kinds of terrain," Marlene pointed out.

"But he didn't bring a crew. Would Jackson go trooping off to hold a measuring stake?"

"Of course not. He would . . . oh, I see what you mean.

William would want to take photographs. Dr. Hayden could take his ground measurements, but it would be more difficult by himself."

"They could be working together, probably are," Slocum said, thinking out loud. "Hayden would tell Jackson what to photograph, take measurements of some of the land, then would have actual pictures without having to measure it on foot."

"You mean he would use William's photos to actually make a map? I've never heard of such a thing. It could speed up the survey."

"Hayden uses his traditional methods when he can, does the mapping off the photographs when he can't."

The smell of sulfur caused Slocum's nose to wrinkle. Yellowstone was festooned with geysers and impassable terrain that Hayden undoubtedly wanted to survey. The combination of techniques could change the way the inhospitable land was mapped.

"What does that mean for finding them?" Marlene asked.

"The terrain not suitable for a wagon would be ignored," Slocum said. "The lowlands would be passed through in favor of elevated overlooks."

He surveyed the horizon. For a brief excursion intended to last only a half day, they had traveled a great distance. Slocum estimated several miles of riding to reach the next high point. What had lured the men on?

Only one reason came to mind.

"The combination of photographs and survey using a transit works," Slocum declared. "They couldn't stop, like a kid playing with a new toy."

"That certainly describes William," Marlene said. "But Dr. Hayden never struck me as the sort who allowed enthusiasm to carry him away from reality."

Slocum didn't know the expedition leader, but he thought Marlene was dead wrong. Hayden's zest for his work knew no bounds. He might keep that light hidden under a bushel basket better than Jackson, but it was there. Slocum had heard it in the man's voice when he spoke of merely traveling through Yellowstone. To be the man responsible for mapping the vast territory would ensure him a place in history.

"There aren't many of the geysers here. Pits there and there," he said, pointing them out. "The broad area between them is likely where a wagon could travel without difficulty."

"It looks dangerous," she said dubiously, but she followed Slocum along the route he had chosen.

Slocum hunted for any trace of the two men. A few ruts might have been left by the darkroom wagon, but he couldn't tell. The constant activity of the mud pools and the recent rains had obliterated real evidence. Then he spotted it.

"They came this way," he said with assurance. "Horse flop. It's likely fresh if you dig down under the hard mud covering." Even as he spoke, a nearby mud pool burbled and belched steaming mud a few feet in the air. "If that pool really spewed out mud, it would cover this track."

"I'm not so sure," Marlene said. "It could be an artifact of the constant eruptions and just looks like, uh, horse manure." She dismounted.

Slocum watched as she took a rock and poked at the pile. She jumped back when the mud coating broke, revealing the soft interior. Marlene looked up in outrage when he laughed.

"Mr. Know-it-all." She threw the rock into the bubbling mud pool and recoiled when it produced a loud, liquid burp as it sank out of sight.

"It won't explode because you tossed a rock in," Slocum assured her. "It's not good to stay too long here, though. The sulfur is making the horses nervous." For his part, he wanted to get out of the mud flats, too. The lowlands wouldn't give them any more spoor. Only spotting Hayden and Jackson from a knoll would allow them to join up.

They struggled up the hill with its soft earth. Slocum saw

where the wagon had worked its way up by following the contours, not daring to attack the hill going straight up the slope. When they crested the hillock, Marlene let out a cry of joy.

"There, John, even I can make out the tracks. They aren't far ahead. But where are they?"

He looked over the increasingly volcanic area and had no idea. It was as if the men and their wagon had vanished from the face of the earth.

17

"Let's head toward the mountains," Slocum said. He chewed on his lower lip as he tried to reconcile this with going after the actual tracks left by the wagon.

"Why, that's not where William and Dr. Hayden drove. Is this a shortcut?" She sounded doubtful, and he didn't blame her.

"Feeling in my gut," he said. "Something's not right, and going the same way will get us into trouble." Slocum looked at the high mountain peaks and the roiling black clouds building there.

The rainy season had been active, but nothing out of the ordinary. The thunderstorms had been mild, never dumping water on his head for more than a few hours. Nevertheless, something about the look of the new cloud buildup worried him.

"I'm going after them," Marlene said. "They can't be that far ahead. You said so yourself."

The distant crack of thunder made him look at the mountains again. In only a few minutes, the lead-bottomed clouds had turned turbulent, building with great speed and rising fast to form the anvil-headed clouds that warned of a real downpour.

"We need to get to high ground and find shelter. That storm's going to be a real frog strangler."

"If we get to the darkroom wagon, we can shelter there," Marlene said. She urged her horse along the ruts still faintly visible on the ground.

Slocum was not worried about failing to see the men or the wagon. That simply meant they were more distant than an easy ride. The storm would hit before they could find Hayden and Jackson anyway. A single heavy droplet spattering against his hat brim warned of that.

He could let Marlene go on her way. She might even be right about finding the men before the storm hit. Slocum weighed his experience against her stubbornness, then snapped the reins and trotted after her. He caught up less than a hundred yards away.

"I'm glad you saw it my way, John. You see, I have this feeling—"

That was as far as she got before Slocum leaned over and got his arm around her waist. With a mighty heave, he pulled her from the saddle and dropped her belly down in front of him.

"Sorry if the saddle horn's uncomfortable," he said. He grabbed her horse's reins and fastened them to his saddle just in front of his knee. Tying them down proved more difficult because of the way she struggled, kicking and trying to slide away to the ground.

"Let me go!"

"Quiet down," Slocum said, turning his pony and heading in the opposite direction. Another drop hit his hat brim with a loud splat!

"I hate you. You can't stop me from getting back to William."

"No way we'll ever find them if we're dead," Slocum said. More raindrops. He rode faster.

Hanging on to Marlene took more of his attention than he liked. Still, her rear end up in the air was an attractive sight. The thunderhead billowing up faster and faster in the afternoon heat, mixing with the water rising from the mountains, lent speed to his ride. After a while Marlene stopped fighting and only grunted whenever the horse hit a rough patch. The slope turned steeper as he rode. By the time he reached the top of the hill, the rain was falling in sheets.

"We need to get to cover. You see a cave?" Slocum asked.

"How can I? I'm upside down while you ogle my ass!" She sputtered and kicked angrily again.

"A pretty one it is, too, but we need to get out of the storm. If the lowlands flood, we'll be safer here than down there."

"Let me go."

Slocum did as she asked. He wanted to simply drop her but thought better of it, instead easing her down until her feet were planted firmly on the rocky ground. From astride his horse, he looked back where they had been—where they had parted from the wagon trail.

"There they are," Slocum said, pointing. "They drove around the hill and went down into a geyser field."

"I told you we should have gone after them. We'd have joined them by now if you hadn't—"

The roar drowned out the woman's diatribe. Water rushed past, cutting deep ravines as it went. Slocum had chosen the rockiest section of the hill, and this saved them.

"Where'd the water come from?" Marlene cried in horror. "That's a tidal wave! It's hardly raining here."

Slocum wasn't exactly sure what a tidal wave was, but if such a thing existed, this was it.

"When it rains in the mountains, it runs off rock. There're a couple hundred square miles of rock that won't suck up any rain. An inch of rain on a hundred square miles of mountain gives you a flood."

The roaring rivers on either side of their hill drowned

out Marlene's reply. Slocum dismounted and looked around for shelter. He had hoped to get deep enough into the foothills to find a cave. They hadn't gone that far. The best chance they had to ride out the storm was a half circle of boulders around a sandy pit that might suck up water.

"Do you have a slicker?"

"No, you didn't say anything about bringing one."

Slocum found one folded and crammed in his saddlebags. He let the wind snap it away to get the wrinkles out. Then he led the horses into the shelter of the towering boulders, found the lee side, and sat down. He waited for Marlene. When she didn't move, letting herself be pelted with increasingly frantic raindrops, he pulled the slicker up over his head and held it out with his right arm to give her the choice. Join him or get very wet.

A sharp crack of distant thunder and a new lightning bolt that blasted across the sky, almost overhead, made her jump. With some reluctance, she settled down in the sand beside him. He lowered the yellow slicker but didn't let her pull it away from him.

"We share or you get wet."

"Already wet," she muttered. She sank into herself, arms tight around her body.

She said something more but the crash of rain hammering down on the rocks around them smothered any words. Slocum found it almost impossible to think of anything but the incessant sound—until Marlene snuggled closer and drew the slicker down in an attempt to keep from getting wetter than she already was. Her warm body pressed into his, and Slocum slowly drifted to sleep, lulled by her nearness and the rain.

He came awake with a start when the downpour slackened. Marlene still slept, but Slocum lifted the edge of the yellow raincoat and peered into the arena where they had taken refuge. His hunch had proven right. Not only had the rain turned into a dangerous storm, but the sandy area had soaked up the water and kept them from having to scramble for even higher ground. The horses were drenched, as was their gear, but Slocum counted himself lucky that they hadn't been trapped out on the plains and swept away in the sudden runoff.

Rearranging the slicker, he slipped out from under, leaving Marlene asleep. Pulling his hat down to protect his eyes from the continuing rainfall, he worked his way out of the protected area. Wind whipped at him, forcing him to grab the Stetson before it blew all the way to Nebraska. The twin rivers formed in the mountains still poured torrents of water on either side of the hilltop, but the speed had decreased.

The flood had come before the rain began in earnest where they stood, so now the storm-fed streams were shrinking. The storm in the mountains had run its course. Slocum knew the one overhead would die down soon, too.

"Can you see them? Or is the rain still too hard?" Marlene moved up behind him. Her arms circled his body as she pulled herself close.

"Lightening," Slocum said. "Storm'll pass soon enough, but there's no way to find them yet."

"You were right. We would have drowned if we'd tried to reach them," she said. "Those rivers are moving too fast for even a horse to ford."

They stood there another few minutes as the storm finally broke and late afternoon sunlight slanted down across Yellowstone. They both spotted the darkroom wagon at the same instant.

"The wagon is askew," Marlene said. "Do you think it washed down off the hill?"

"Looks to be the case," Slocum said. The wagon was tipped on its side as if it had slid a ways downhill before toppling over. Hayden and Jackson had had the sense to seek higher ground, for all the good it had done them. Still, if they had stayed on the hill, they'd be wet but alive.

"Can we start out now? I'm worried about them."

Slocum peered up at the sky. The lightning had stopped

lancing across the sky. He didn't hear any thunder, near or distant, and the rain was slackening. He nodded. In twenty minutes they picked their way down the hill where they had ridden out the storm, and in an hour they were struggling up the far side of the hill where they had seen the wagon.

"They aren't here," Marlene said as they crested the rise. "They must have already gone to right the wagon."

Slocum didn't voice his concern. If the men had been in the wagon when it began sliding down the hillside, they might be trapped inside. With all the noxious chemicals Jackson used as a photographer, they might have been burned or suffocated.

"Stay here. It looks slippery from all the rain."

Marlene said nothing as Slocum handed her the reins, hitched up his gun belt, then turned sideways to brake his slide as much as possible. For all his preparation, he still lost his balance and went sliding downhill on his side. The ground was almost liquid from the rain. He suspected the constant downpour of sulfur and other chemicals from the nearby geysers had altered the earth, too.

That mattered less to him than slamming into the bottom of the overturned wagon. He fetched up hard, then got to his feet using the wagon as support.

"Jackson? Hayden? You here?"

He heard a low moan and made his way toward the wagon. When he reached the back of it, he saw how Jackson had caught his leg beneath a wheel.

"You break anything?" Slocum asked him.

"It's good to see you, too, sir," Jackson said. He winced and tugged with both hands on his leg. "I cannot tell, but it wouldn't surprise me."

"Where's Hayden?"

"He went the rest of the way downhill to find a limb or something to use as a splint. I fear that I will need it when I dig out from underneath this fiasco."

"You shouldn't have tried to keep the wagon from sliding

down," Slocum said as he dropped beside the photographer and examined the man's leg. He had seen his share of compound fractures. He had to get the man out from under the wagon before he tried setting this one.

"How did you know? The rain had started. I felt the wagon shift and jumped out, thinking a shove against the down side would keep it upright."

"It toppled on you and all that kept you from getting crushed to death was the soft ground. You're one lucky son of a bitch."

Slocum got his hands around the wheel and tested it. With a bit of back-and-forth he worried a space beneath the wheel, then heaved.

Jackson saw what he tried and was ready. As Slocum lifted the wagon wheel a bare inch, the photographer threw himself backward and skidded a few feet before stopping. His howl of pain could have been heard in Saint Louis.

Slocum controlled his own slide down and stopped by the man. The bone thrusting through Jackson's flesh and pant leg gleamed whitely.

"Going to set this right now. Bite down on your sleeve. This is going to hurt like hell."

Slocum put one boot against Jackson's inner thigh, gripped the broken leg with both hands, and applied slow, even pressure. He wasn't sure when the photographer passed out, but it let him finish the job. The broken bone vanished back under the cloth and into the skin. A distinct snap convinced Slocum the leg bone was back where it belonged. Depending on how clean the break was, Jackson might not even walk with a limp after it healed.

"Mr. Slocum!"

"I didn't think he could wait for you to set his leg."

Hayden held up two sturdy limbs he had fetched for the splint.

"I couldn't get him out from under the wagon. I wanted to use these as a lever."

"Splint him up. He'll come around soon enough and will want to walk." Slocum flopped back on the muddy grass and stared into the still cloudy sky. It had been a hell of a day so far.

"Dr. Hayden, is he all right?" Marlene rode up from the downslope. She hadn't waited but had gone around the hill, where it was nowhere as steep as this side.

"Mr. Slocum came to the rescue again. Set the leg as good as I could have."

"I doubt that," Marlene said skeptically.

"Help me bind him up. When he wakes, we'll see how good the job actually was."

They carried Jackson to the foot of the hill, where Marlene tended him. A fire helped dry them out while Slocum and Hayden made their way back up the hillside to the wagon.

"Anything dangerous get spilled?" Slocum asked.

"I believe William had everything well secured. What are we going to do about the wagon?"

Slocum looked downhill, kicked at the loose sod, and then said, "Push it all the way to the bottom. Can't do any more harm than's been done already. Where'd the team get off to?"

"We had unharnessed them before the wagon began its unfortunate descent."

Slocum considered that a good thing. If they got the wagon back on its wheels, he didn't cotton much to pushing it back to the expedition camp. His horse and Marlene's would balk at being used as draft animals after being ridden.

"Stay clear," Slocum said, hunkering down and getting his shoulder into the top of the wagon. Straightening his legs and heaving got the wagon slipping a little.

When Hayden added his weight, the wagon began sliding of its own accord.

"Look out below!" Slocum called. "There's no stopping it till it gets to the bottom."

He and Hayden slipped and slid down behind it. The wagon came to a halt at a perfect spot. Slocum needed only to dig at the soft dirt under the wheels on the down side. This added help might allow them to push the wagon up onto its wheels.

It had seemed like a good plan, but Slocum finally hooked a rope around the top of the wagon and had Marlene lead both their horses away, pulling hard while he and Hayden got under and pushed until the wagon creaked and groaned upright on its wheels.

"I'll scout for the team. They wouldn't have run far in the rain." And they hadn't. Slocum found both horses less than a mile to the east, near one of the noxious sulfur pools.

He led them away, found sweet water, and let the horses drink. By the time he had returned to the wagon, Marlene had cleaned up the inside of spilled chemicals and Jackson lay propped on a blanket.

"You've done me a great service, Mr. Slocum," the photographer said. "We need to return to camp, but afterward you can do me another great service."

Slocum glanced at Marlene, who beamed.

"What is it?" he asked suspiciously.

"I want you to become the expedition's official photographer."

Slocum had done about everything possible roaming the West. He had never been a photographer, however.

"I wouldn't know what to do."

"Miss Wilkes will show you."

Slocum heard a voice agreeing to the cockamamie plan, then realized it was his own.

18

"You're catching on fast, John," Marlene said, standing close behind him, her arms reaching around to adjust the camera.

"It's not that hard," he said. Between Jackson and Marlene, he had learned how to operate the camera within a day's time.

The most difficult part was being careful with the photographic plates. The unexposed ones were fragile and susceptible to light leaking through the black paper and metal slides holding them. Once in the camera, the exposure wasn't too hard to figure out, depending on the amount of sun. Taking care of the exposed plate required him to reverse the process.

"You won't have to develop the photographs. William is able to do that since he can sit on a stool while he works in the darkroom."

"I don't see any reason not to spend the rest of the day taking photographs," Slocum said, aware that Marlene had edged a tad closer to him. The feel of her moving against him was turning him hard in the crotch. There wouldn't be much photography done, but all Jackson or Hayden needed was a photograph every few miles along the expedition's route.

Hayden used them for his survey work, and Jackson considered them artistry. Slocum wasn't certain he held up that end of the chore, but with Marlene along, this was another thing that hardly mattered to him.

They had traveled through some gorgeous country and were pushing into the northwesternmost section of Yellowstone. He had enjoyed the photography and the scouting. He had even found himself getting along with the fussy Gustav Leroq.

The artist worried Slocum more than anything else. The Blackfoot trouble was long behind them, the rains had slowed in frequency and intensity, and the route through the geyser fields had proved easy. The terrain was now almost totally devoid of the bubbling springs or exploding fountains of steam and boiling water. But what should he do about Leroq? The artist had stolen Sean Innick's property, and the ruby was long lost. From the furious pace Leroq worked, he must have gone through the entire jar of ruby dust by now and would begin using the amethyst soon to enhance his paints.

He ought to be returned to Otter Creek and Marshal Smith's jail for trial. But what would that accomplish? Leroq wasn't a thief in any sense Slocum had run across before. The man thought he needed the precious stones to create art. He didn't sell them to go on a bender or gamble away the price of the ruby. He didn't even use the gemstone to dazzle a soiled dove. He used it for his work.

That didn't absolve him of the theft. And that worried at Slocum like a hunting dog with a treed squirrel.

"We're about done with the work for the day," Slocum said.

"Then let's get the plates back to William so he can examine them. Dr. Hayden is anxious since we are so near the end of our trip."

"Near the end," Slocum said, rolling the idea over in his head. What would he do after the expedition disbanded? Hayden and his crew would return to Washington with their fancy maps.

"Yes, William and I are going to Boston. He has an exhibition scheduled for the finest of the photographs. Some of yours must be included, John. Come with us. Come back and you'll be the talk of the town!"

Slocum could imagine how he would be the talk of Boston high society. Marlene would fit right in. Put her in a fancy gown, and with her fine manners, she would charm them to death. Slocum doubted they would let him wear his Colt. That didn't bother him too much. He had spent long nights gambling at the Union Club in San Francisco, decked out in a tuxedo. But there he had carried a derringer and a knife, just in case.

He closed the case and handed it to Marlene.

"I'll get the tripod and camera."

She bounced about joyously, her dreams bubbling like one of the hot water ponds they had passed.

"We're not fifty miles from Montana," Slocum said. "I saw it on one of Hayden's old maps."

"We're going to Missoula Mills, then we'll start our journey back to the East."

"Hayden said that," Slocum muttered. The expedition was nearing an end, forcing him to come to more decisions than what to do about Leroq.

"Let's not worry about that now. We still have a week or more. Much more if William wants to finish shooting all the plates. He was hoarding them, worrying that something even more scenic would come by. We can now afford to shoot with abandon."

"*He* ought to be doing it," Slocum complained.

"Nonsense, John. You're doing a fine job."

Slocum knew that without her sharp eye for angle and composition, his photographs would have been worthless to

Hayden or Jackson. If anything, Marlene was the real photographer, and he did little more than click the shutter when she told him to.

They rode back to the camp where the expedition had stayed for several days. He saw that Leroq and his wagon were gone. He called to Fenwicke, "Is Leroq out drawing his pictures again?"

"He said as much when he pulled out this morning. Wanted first light or something like that. Never could quite understand his exasperation at poor light. If you can see, it's good light. Yes, that's it, good light."

Fenwicke walked away talking to himself.

"He's a strange duck," Marlene said.

"So's Leroq. At least Fenwicke doesn't steal precious stones that I know of."

"His habits are even more curious, I am sure," Marlene said, leaving Slocum to wonder what those might be. He had spent little time with many of the expedition members. When he wasn't working for Jackson, he was scouting for Hayden. The loss of the other two scouts had placed a heavier burden on him.

Before, he wouldn't have minded being alone on the trail. Now he felt it took him away from Marlene. No warm, willing body stretched next to his under the blanket at night made him eager to finish his scouting work and return.

They reached the darkroom wagon as Jackson opened the door. The man beamed when he saw Marlene. She handed up the case with the newly exposed photographic plates.

"Wait for me to develop and print these. I need to know if more of the same terrain are needed or if you can move on."

"We'll be here, William," she said.

Slocum saw the photographer's look and knew more than photography was on the man's mind.

"Let's get something to eat, John. It will be a while. William really should teach you how to develop the plates. The real artistry comes in the printing, finding the right focus and section of each plate."

"There's a lot of artistry around these parts," Slocum said, looking at her. She actually blushed.

They didn't say much as they had their noonday meal and went back to find Jackson sitting on the lower step of the darkroom wagon. He held up one of the photographs.

"Excellent work, sir. You have quite the eye. I should hire you as my assistant."

"No need," Slocum said. "Marlene is the one who chose the angle. All I did was pull the lanyard on the camera. She did all the setup."

"Nonsense," Jackson said. "A woman cannot see such framing, such composition. Not like a man. You have done well, Mr. Slocum."

"I set your leg," Slocum said. "I'm thinking I ought to take part of that splint and beat some sense into your head."

"What?" Jackson looked up, startled. He had been leafing through the new photographs.

"Marlene is the one responsible for any artistry. I carried the equipment and didn't do much else."

"You are too modest, sir. Too modest by half. Finish your work. I look forward—"

"To seeing how Miss Wilkes has given you more masterpieces," Slocum interrupted him.

Jackson looked at him strangely and hobbled back into the darkroom. He shut the door with a click. Slocum put his foot on the lower step, intending to pull the photographer from his lair and pound sense into him when Marlene took his arm and held him back.

"It's all right, John. You don't need to take my part."

"You did the work." Slocum wasn't sure pointing the camera in the right direction to get a good picture constituted work, but it was something he couldn't do. He might take a dozen pictures—or a hundred—and get only one that carried the startling grandeur of most of Marlene's.

"William knows. He's just a little slow to come around to admitting it in public. Women aren't supposed to know these things."

"If he knows, then it won't be any trouble for him to come out and say it."

"Let's go, John. We have some time to find a place to capture the geyser fields to the north at sunset. The lighting then will be perfect."

"I don't understand things like that. I can rope, hog-tie, and brand a calf. I can—"

"John, come along." The way she spoke settled Slocum's ire. A little. It wasn't right for him to take any credit for Marlene's work, yet Jackson was intent on just that.

They packed more unexposed plates, some victuals, and rode a few miles beyond the spot where they had spent the morning taking photographs. When Marlene drew rein and studied the landscape ahead, Slocum had to admit the view was spectacular. As she had ridden, the top buttons on her blouse had come unfastened, giving him a hint of breast. The thin white slice of bare flesh bobbed about delightfully as she turned suddenly to face him.

She saw the focus of his gaze and her hand flew to cover the bare skin.

"Are you enjoying the sight?"

"I am," Slocum said. His green eyes rose to meet her brown ones.

She smiled slowly. Her hand no longer hid the momentary indiscretion. Instead, she flicked her fingers and opened two more buttons. Then another. She drew her shoulders back and pulled the cloth taut. When she relaxed, the blouse fell open all the way down the front, almost to her navel. Marlene reached up and pulled down her right sleeve. Slowly, she pulled down her left and shucked off her blouse. She wore only a thin undergarment. Slocum saw the hard nipples poking into the cloth, betraying her arousal.

"We have to wait for the light," she said. "That might be an hour. However shall we pass the time?"

"Not on horseback," Slocum said, stepping down. He fastened the reins around a low bush. By the time he turned back to Marlene, she had stepped out of her skirt and stood silhouetted by the sun.

The movement of her limbs, the way she half turned and let him get an outline of her breasts, made him harder. Slocum dropped his gun belt, tossed his Stetson aside, and began stripping off his coat, vest, and shirt. The more he removed, the heavier Marlene's breathing came. He was turning her on by his slow revealing of bare flesh as much as she was by her nakedness.

"Now, John, no more teasing," she said, coming to him. She pulled off the last of her clothing, naked from the top of her head down to her shoes.

Slocum dropped his jeans and let his manhood spring out, jutting proudly between them. She caught the shaft and started to bend to take it. He held her upright. His hand pressed into her belly until it began to heave in response. Only then did he move lower. His finger curled about and entered her. She cried out, closed her eyes, and threw her head back. The wind caught her long, brunette hair and whipped it around like a banner.

Slocum moved a little closer and added a second finger to stir about in her wet, hot depths. His palm pressed down hard into her mons. His other hand circled her and grasped her taut buttocks. The flow of her unclad body under his hands thrilled him, made him pulse and throb with arousal that threatened to rob him of control.

His fingers slipped from her wet slit.

"No, no, that felt so good," she complained.

"This will feel better," he promised.

He got down on his knees, reached through her legs, then stood. She let out a yelp of surprise. Her rump pushed hard into his erection as her ankles rested on his shoulders. He held her bent double like this, then began bouncing her up and down. She got the idea and reached around to guide him into the target they both wanted hit.

They groaned in desire as he slipped far into her. Bent double as she was allowed even deeper penetration. The power of his arms as he held her let her surrender fully to him. Slocum controlled everything. He swung about as he lifted her away, only to let her sink back.

The blood pounded in Slocum's temples as he began to speed up the motion that drove his fleshy shaft balls deep into her center. He felt her gripping down all around his hidden length, massaging, coaxing out the white-hot lava boiling in his loins.

He pulled her tightly to his body. Her breasts crushed against her upper thighs. Marlene had reached up so her fingers laced behind his head for added support. He kissed her hard as she bounced up and down. Sweat dribbled between her breasts. Slocum tried to snare it with his tongue but failed. He returned to kissing her. When her lips parted slightly, his tongue invaded her mouth just as he entered her nether lips far lower.

The tensions mounted until Slocum could hold back no longer. Just as he cried out and spilled his load, she gasped and her inner muscles tensed all around him, milking him, trying to crush him flat. They rode out their passions, locked in desire, and eventually the intense moment passed. She dropped first one leg and then the other while he continued to support her by gripping her ass cheeks.

Even after both her feet were solidly planted on the ground, they remained pressed together, not saying a word, simply enjoying the warm afterglow of their sexual release. Their sweat glued them together, Slocum's broad chest to her breasts. And then they parted.

"Time to photograph beauty," she said.

"I've already seen it," he said, kissing her. It was almost twilight before they got around to taking the photographs of the landscape.

19

"Excellent photographs, Mr. Slocum. You have quite the eye." Jackson leafed through the prints, barely dry, that Marlene had taken the day before just as night fell.

They had been late returning to the camp, but no one noticed. There was a nervous energy that drove all the members now. The survey expedition neared its end and each had a great deal of work to do. Cartographers toiled over creating new maps, complete with elevation lines, and Hayden struggled to coordinate it all. Jackson had gratefully accepted the dual role of photographing the land to be translated into paper maps as well as a more artistic pursuit of capturing Yellowstone's beauty. He had almost abandoned the work using a paintbrush, leaving that to Gustav Leroq.

"Marlene is responsible."

"I'm sure she did all she could to assist you. Oh, there is only a week or two left. We have no time to waste. I want you to go out again. Dr. Hayden wants pictures, of course, but you need to concentrate on the vistas to the east and north. You—"

"There you are, Mr. Slocum." Hayden walked so fast he

almost ran. "We are in quite a dilemma, one only you can resolve."

"I say, Ferdinand, I simply cannot spare him right now. There is great need to—"

"To scout or we will be stranded here for weeks, weeks for which we have no supplies and will never be reimbursed by the government," Hayden said. "We must know the best route, either to the northeast or the northwest. There are a considerable number of geysers directly in our path."

"I can scout it," Slocum said. "Miss Wilkes is capable of taking the photographs for Jackson."

"Glad to hear it, yes, glad," Hayden said, his mind already moving on to other problems. "So little time. You're right about that, William, so right. We have to all do double duty."

"Then Slocum can take a camera and shoot pictures while he is scouting." Jackson looked smug.

Slocum saw how excited Marlene looked at the chance to work on her own. The only reason they had gone out together was for him to carry the equipment. She could do that. He scotched the photographer's demand immediately.

"I have to travel fast if I'm to scout both routes," he said. "Carrying fifty pounds of camera, tripod, and plates will slow me quite a bit. It'd add an extra week to the survey."

"No camera, just scout," Hayden said definitively. He rushed away to tend to some trivial problem Fenwicke had found and couldn't deal with on his own.

"I can ride with you partway," Slocum said.

"But she can't do the quality of work you have."

"She can, she will," Slocum said. He didn't give Jackson the chance to argue further. He either sent Marlene out or didn't get his pictures.

When Slocum had stuffed all the supplies he could into his saddlebags to keep from having to forage along the way, he looked up and saw Marlene beaming at him. She was already mounted and waiting for him.

"Thank you, John. He will find fault with all my pictures, but I will give him the finest ones possible."

"You've got as much talent as he has," Slocum said. "What it'll take to make him see that . . ." He let his words trail off as he shook his head. With a quick step, foot in the stirrup, he mounted and headed north from the expedition camp. Marlene rode alongside.

They never spoke of their intimate time together, gingerly avoiding any such suggestions or speculation when they might again spend the night together. When they reached the geysers that worried Hayden, Slocum said, "Looks like a wagon set out to the northwest."

"Gustav," she said, "left early this morning. He feels the rush as much as anyone else. It takes a long time for his oils to dry, and he still has an entire carrying case unfilled."

Slocum considered the two routes and knew what he had to do. He leaned over, kissed Marlene, then said, "I'll go after him."

"And I will go in the other direction. There are great views from those hills ahead. The Yellowstone River cuts through them."

"If you listen hard, you can hear a waterfall," Slocum said. Through the hissing and bubbling of the geysers, he caught the telltale sound. "That would make a good photograph."

"A spectacular one." She hesitated, frowned, and then said, "If such a waterfall exists along the river, that's not the way to travel, is it? For the expedition?"

"That's why I'm following Leroq," he said. Reluctantly letting the woman go northeast while he went northwest, Slocum set out.

As he rode, he took notes about the landmarks, the condition of the ground, and what lay ahead. Trying to cross a chasm along the Yellowstone River would be difficult, if not impossible. Since time was a consideration, ferrying wagons across a powerful river meant a week or more Hayden did not wish to expend.

Page after page of notes flowed under his pencil. He wished he had Marlene's talents at sketching. Even possessing Leroq's artistry would have given him more complete notes for Hayden and the rest to follow. Scouting before had been a matter of riding out a day or two, assessing the ease of travel, then reporting back. Now he felt obligated to give as complete a picture as he could of the dangers the expedition faced if they came this way.

In midafternoon, Slocum spotted Leroq in his wagon a mile ahead. The artist struggled to stay on solid ground. More than once he slewed to the side, perilously close to the pools of hot water dotting the land. Slocum took the time to sketch out a route that looked more secure.

When he looked up from his mapmaking, he saw that Leroq had abandoned his wagon and frantically worked to unbridle his team. The wagon wheels on the left side had come to rest in mud. The wagon tilted a little as it slid into boiling water.

Slocum got his pony galloping. The man would only make it worse if he tried to prevent his wagon from sinking deeper. Releasing his team was the smartest thing he did. By the time Slocum came to a halt, Leroq had grabbed on to the side of the wagon where he had firmer footing and tried by strength of arm and back to prevent the wagon from being swallowed whole.

"You can't stop it," Slocum called. He hit the ground and ran to Leroq's side. "There's a suction pulling the wagon in."

"I'll go around and push from the other side!"

"Don't be a fool. The water in that pond's boiling!"

"My paintings! I can't lose them."

Slocum glanced at the wagon bed where the fancy cases were secured against jolting about. This now worked against the artist. If the wagon submerged in the hot water, his paintings, trapped in their specially made crates, would disappear, too. Retrieving them from the pool would be impossible.

"Bring the team around," Slocum ordered. "Do it. Now!" The sharp bite of command had stood him in good stead during the war. He had risen to the rank of captain and had few veterans and many raw recruits toward the end of the war. With training so brief for his men, he had learned to sound positive and never give conflicting orders.

Leroq almost carried the two horses in his haste to bring them around.

"Lash the harness to the side of the wagon, here and here," Slocum said. "Don't worry about it being secure. We won't have to pull but for a minute or two."

The sucking noise as the pond filled with mud and boiling water grew as it swallowed more of the wagon. The left wheels were up to the hubs and sinking faster by the minute.

"Have them pull for all they're worth," Slocum said, jumping up to the side of the wagon. Balancing precariously, he made sure he remembered how the cases had been secured.

He found it harder than staying on a bucking bronc as the wagon skewed even more into the water, splashing him with the blistering water. Slocum ignored this, used his knife, and slashed at the ropes holding the cases.

"Wait, you can't. Don't hurt the paintings!"

Slocum ignored the artist and severed the last of the rope holding the nearest cases. Bracing himself, he hefted one of the heavy cases, arched his back, and heaved. The case sailed through the air and crashed to the ground just beyond Leroq. Working methodically, Slocum heaved out five cases and worked on the remaining sixth when the wheels in the pool broke. The hot water had caused the iron rims to expand. The wood yielded and the wagon tipped completely on its side.

Arms around the last case, Slocum strained to throw

himself up into the air. He felt the wagon disappear under his boots. For an instant he hung suspended. If he had waited too long, he would come down in the boiling water. But unexpected help came. Leroq grabbed for him and, airborne, circled Slocum's body and the bulky case with his flailing arms. Spinning fast, he carried them away from the pond to land in a heap.

For a moment Slocum couldn't breathe. The case had crushed down on his chest, driving out the air. His vision blurred and even trying to suck in the sulfur-laden air tore at his lungs. Then he felt himself being pulled along the ground. He clung to the case with Leroq's paintings, even when a faint voice told him to let go.

"No, can't, gotta save 'em," he gasped out.

"You have saved them. Let me have my paintings, dammit."

Leroq proved stronger than Slocum in his dazed condition. For a long minute Slocum fought to regain his strength. When he did, he saw Leroq moving the cases even farther from the pool—and the wagon was nowhere to be seen.

"It ate it," Leroq said in a small voice. "The pool ate the entire wagon, as if it were nothing but a tasty morsel." He straightened, struck a pose, hand on one lapel, foot forward, and chin high. "You, sir, are my savior. You rescued my art. You are to be congratulated for preserving such artistry to be admired by the entire world!"

Slocum couldn't believe the pool, its water slightly murky with sulfur and other chemicals, could have caused the entire wagon to vanish so completely. He didn't want to find out how deep the pool was, but it had to be farther to the bottom than he could have ever guessed.

He peered over the edge. Deep down the pond looked like a morning glory flower, the same color blue and funnel-shaped. The water bubbled and sizzled all around, but the pool looked only a few feet deep. Then he saw the last vestige of the wagon at the bottom. The size, even taking the magnifying power of the water into account, was so tiny it had to be fifty feet down. Slocum stepped back when the bubbles began rising.

"You gave it indigestion," Slocum said. "Let's get away from here."

"How do I carry my paintings? I will not leave even one of them. They are precious! They—"

Slocum shut out the artist's bragging on how exquisite the paintings were as he set to lashing them onto the two horses from Leroq's team. Throwing a diamond hitch was hard, but he made do. He wished the cases had been constructed with straps, but he did his best with the material at hand.

"Let's go."

"You are my angel, sir, my rescuer, my—"

"Walk." Slocum mounted and led the two horses burdened with the cases. He might have let Leroq ride double, but this way he kept the artist's constant babble at a minimum. When they reached more solid terrain, Slocum tossed the artist the reins to the team.

"I cannot do any more paintings, sir. These are all there will be," Leroq said in sorrow. "My paints went to the bottom of that pool with the wagon."

Slocum knew whatever was left of Innick's ruby had disappeared, too.

"How far had you driven along this route?" Slocum asked. "You were on your way back."

"Several miles. This is the most treacherous portion of my trip. Past this ugly array of boiling lagoons is level, decent land. Gorgeous, but nothing like these pools for sheer artistry."

"So if the expedition gets past these," Slocum said, his arm encompassing the hot water lakes, "it would be easy going?"

"Quite so."

Slocum had mapped out a better way through this volcanic region. Hayden had his route north because Slocum

knew that to the northeast the surging river would pose
grave difficulties to cross. The Yellowstone River must have
formed an oxbow since this way gave no hint of the need to
go past—the expedition could remain on the western side
of the river all the way into Montana.

"Let's get back to camp," Slocum said, a mixture of ela-
tion and sorrow vying for supremacy.

"Excellent work," Dr. Hayden said, leafing through Slocum's
sketches. "We can finish our mapping with these as our
guide."

Slocum barely listened. He looked past the expedition
leader to the darkroom wagon, where Jackson and Marlene
sat on the step, discussing with real animation the photographs she had taken of the river and waterfall. From everything Marlene had said, that route would be difficult,
requiring more than one crossing of the river. Going farther
west gave the expedition a far easier trip.

"I would like you to scout farther, though, just to be on
the safe side."

"My work's done," Slocum said. "I need to go back to Otter
Creek." He hadn't recovered Innick's ruby but had to tell the
man it was lost. It didn't much matter if Innick thought he
had stolen the ruby for himself and was inclined to go on a
bender with the proceeds from the sale, but more than reputation was at stake.

Slocum had promised to retrieve the ruby and had to let
Innick and his wife know he had failed. What details he
provided were something he could mull over on his way
back to Utah.

"But another week! Until we reach Missoula Mills, your
services can be useful."

"Useful, not really needed, though."

"I'll pay you another hundred dollars. A week's work."

"That's mighty generous, but I have another commit-
ment." Slocum would be denied the five-hundred-dollar

reward for recovering the ruby, but the money didn't matter. He had promised Innick.

"Very well, sir. You are an excellent worker. If you require a letter of recommendation, please feel free to ask me. There are sure to be other expeditions through this area, and your expertise would be invaluable."

"If you can wire my pay to Salt Lake City, I can pick it up there."

"Yes, yes, that is satisfactory. Very." Hayden turned his head and was already casting about for a new problem to solve.

Slocum thanked him and went to Jackson's wagon. He had barely gotten within polite speaking distance when Jackson piped up, "Slocum! Look at these. Marvelous work done by my assistant. Miss Wilkes has talents I never recognized before."

"Do tell," he said dryly. Slocum didn't miss how Marlene hung on to Jackson's arm.

"He's going to give me credit at the Boston show, John. And there is another expedition, this one in the Appalachians, where William is certain to be hired to take more photographs. He's told me I can come along as his primary assistant."

"You deserve it," Slocum said. He started to bid her farewell but Marlene chattered on about the opportunity this afforded her and how certain Jackson was of being received as a master photographer in Boston society.

"I've got to talk to Leroq." He touched the brim of his dirty, battered hat.

"Oh, yes, fine, John." She turned back to her employer, who basked in the adoration she gave.

Slocum had done what he could to say good-bye. He went to the far side of the camp, where Leroq had opened the cases to examine every painting for damage.

"Slocum, sir! Not a one has been harmed. Well, except one. How this happened is something of a mystery since the oil dried some time ago." He held up the painting Slocum had examined what seemed an eternity back. His fingerprint on the corner marred it for Leroq. Slocum hardly noticed, though he did hold up his thumb to see if any of the paint remained. It had long since worn off.

"I would like to gift you with this painting. It's not up to the standards of the others, not with this smudge in the corner. Without my paints, I cannot remedy it. Here, take it for your trouble."

Leroq thrust the painting out to Slocum, who took it, not knowing what to do with it.

The artist stared hard at Slocum, then asked, "Are you going to insist on returning me to that dreary place over the matter of the purloined ruby?"

"Buy your material, don't steal it," Slocum said.

He took the painting, found his horse, and lashed his reward to the hindquarters. The horse didn't like the painting bouncing about so Slocum pried the painting loose from its frame and rolled it up. The horse liked this better.

So did Slocum as he hit the trail for Utah.

20

Otter Creek hadn't changed one whit since Slocum had left over a month earlier. As he rode down the main street, faint sounds of the sawmill outside town echoed down the valley and across the rapidly running stream. He paused outside the marshal's office. The day was hot and Smith had left the door open to catch the faint breeze. Just inside, the marshal leaned back in his chair, his feet hiked to the desk and his hat pulled down to shade his eyes. He snored as loud as the big saw tearing through wood. Slocum heard the lawman all the way out in the street.

He rode past. Curious eyes followed him but no one greeted him now. He had been gone long enough that he was no longer considered a local, if he ever had been. At least earlier, when he worked for Sean Innick, the tradesmen spoke to him, just in case he had the boss's ear and could buy a little extra from them with each supply trip into town.

A dozen times on the ride to the sawmill, Slocum told himself there was no need for him to report his failure to retrieve the ruby. He still had a fair amount of the original reward for recouping most of Mrs. Innick's jewelry. There hadn't been that many places to spend money out in the middle of the Yellowstone wilderness. A bottle or two of whiskey and a few dollars spent along the way had been mostly recovered in late-night card games with the expedition staff. They might have had a great deal of book learning but were far from being the best poker players he had encountered west of the Mississippi.

Hitching his horse a ways from Innick's office, he looked up at the sawmill where Reese had lost his arm and his life. Innick had promised a decent gravestone. Slocum needed to check to see if the owner had kept his word. But that could wait.

Until after . . .

"Never thought to see your face here again, Slocum," Tomasson said, huffing and puffing as he made his way down the steep hill from the saw. "You fixin' to work again? I got need of a mechanic on the water wheel. Damned thing keeps seizin' up. Needs more than bear grease on its axle."

"Is Innick there?" Slocum pointed toward the small cabin the owner used as his office.

"Nah, him and the missus are in the house. Ain't seen much of 'em the past week or so."

"Why's that?" Slocum saw the nasty grin on the foreman's face.

"Why don't you go on up to the house and ask?" Tomasson went away laughing.

That told Slocum something dire had happened and just asking would bring down a towering wrath on his head. Coupled with his failure to recover the ruby and bring back its thief didn't bode well. He worked a few seconds at his gear, then tucked the painting under his arm. As he climbed up the hilltop to the owner's house, Slocum knew there was damned little Innick could do to him. He had most of the first reward to help him along the trail. Hayden was wiring his pay from scouting for the expedition to Salt Lake City. And even with Tomasson and a half-dozen others from the mill, Innick wasn't going to stop Slocum when he chose to leave.

That buoyed Slocum's spirits. What could Innick do?

He rapped sharply on the door and stepped back, waiting impatiently. A servant opened the door and looked at him with eyes as wide as a fawn caught by a hunter.

"You must go," she said, glancing over her shoulder. "This is not a good time for business."

"Tell Mr. Innick it's about the stolen ruby."

The maid turned even paler, then asked in a hoarse voice, "It is good news? He needs good news."

"It's not."

"Then go. Please."

"Mary, who's at the door?"

Slocum recognized Mrs. Innick's voice. She didn't sound any happier than everyone made her husband out to be.

"It is the man sent to get your ruby."

"Don't just stand there, show him in. Immediately!"

Slocum wanted to reassure the maid it would be all right, that he would be the lightning rod of the Innicks' anger, but he knew it wouldn't work that way. He could leave. The maid was forced to endure whatever storm Slocum released.

"You found it!" Mrs. Innick came to him, then slowed when she saw his expression. "Don't tell me you failed to bring it back."

"That's right, ma'am." Slocum heard a distant door hinge creak. In a few seconds Sean Innick boiled into the room, face florid and his hands clenched into fists as if he prepared to go a hundred rounds bare knuckle.

"You didn't even catch the thief, did you, Slocum?"

"No, sir," Slocum said. He tried not to feel too happy at delivering the bad news. A promise made ought to have been a promise kept, but circumstances had prevented him from delivering. "The ruby was lost in a geyser. In Yellowstone."

"You tracked the thief all the way into the Yellowstone?" Innick obviously didn't believe him.

"The thief is somewhere in Montana now, but the ruby is at the bottom of a pool of boiling water and mud."

"You didn't try to drain it?"

"Oh, Sean, the boy said it was a pond of boiling water. How do you drain something like that? I've heard of those pools and geysers and things."

"I'm sorry you won't be able to give it to your daughter on her wedding day." Slocum almost stepped back when he saw how both of them turned completely furious at that.

"Dear Laura is *not* getting married," Mrs. Innick said.

"That dog in the manger she was going to marry left her to prospect for gold in Virginia City. Just upped and left her," Mr. Innick added.

Slocum wanted to ask if there had been more to it. Having in-laws like the Innicks would send any man out into the desert or mountains to be all by his lonesome.

"That's a shame. I brought a painting for her wedding present. Might be you can put it to use. It's by a painter known for his landscapes. Gustav Leroq is a famous artist." He unrolled the painting and held it up for Mrs. Innick to see.

"Why, it is gorgeous. Fine art! And see how it sparkles, Sean. It's as if the landscape is catching the light and reflecting it so it is even brighter."

"A real gem," Slocum said.

"You're giving this to us?" Sean Innick sounded dubious. "That doesn't mean I have to pay you. You didn't recover the ruby."

"Oh, forget the stone, Sean. I can put this up on the wall where the ladies can see it when they come for tea. It was done by a famous artist?"

"Very famous," Slocum assured her.

"Give him what you said you'd pay for getting back the ruby. This is ever so much higher class."

"The artist is on his way back to Boston for an exhibit. High-society event, he said." Slocum had no idea if Leroq had gone with William Jackson and Marlene or if he was heading for different parts. He had learned from Leroq that the painting mattered less than the story that went with it.

"Pay him, Sean," Mrs. Innick said. "I see we need to go to that cabinet maker in town and have him make a suitable frame."

"Dillingham," Slocum said. "His work is top-notch."

Innick fumbled in his pocket and pulled out a roll of paper money. He leafed through it, discarding some notes and choosing others. He thrust the bills at Slocum.

"There. All on a Salt Lake City bank."

Slocum knew better than ask for specie. Besides, he had to go to Salt Lake City anyway to collect the rest of his money from Hayden. He backed away, then almost ran from the house and down the hill to his horse. Where he went now didn't matter. He had a better poke than he'd carried in years.

With his horse under him, he considered heading back north. To Montana. Missoula Mills, Hayden had said. Marlene would be there. With William Jackson and the promise of fame for her photographic work hanging alongside his.

Marlene.

The name rolled off his tongue, echoed in his head, and caused tremors in his crotch, but like the ruby, she was lost to him. One had disappeared as dust into a volcanic pool. And the woman would be swallowed up by high society in Boston. Where she belonged.

Slocum headed southwest toward Salt Lake City. From there he could ride east. There might be a rancher or two in Colorado, in Middle Park, who needed a wrangler. That was where he belonged.

Watch for

SLOCUM AND THE SNAKE-PIT SLAVERS

412th novel in the exciting SLOCUM series
from Jove

Coming in June!